WARNING

This book contains sexually explicit scenes and adult language. It may be considered offensive to some readers. This book is for sale to adults ONLY.

* * * * * * * * * * * * * * * * * * *

Please store your files wisely where they cannot be accessed by underage readers.

ISBN-13: 978-1988083797
ISBN-10: 1988083796

Other books by Shyla Starr:

<u>Persuasive Billionaire BWWM Romance Series</u>

Stacey is trying to keep a handle on her life the best that she can. She is on the verge of losing her job and her apartment, while taking care of her sick grandmother. Her life takes an unexpected turn when she meets Charlie, who works for the construction company that is attempting to persuade her to move out of her home.

<u>Elusive Billionaire Romance Series</u>

Billionaire Hendrick is trying to repair his company's image by putting in some volunteer work, building a school and hospital for the impoverished children in Africa. There, he meets a beautiful African American volunteer, Jocelyn. They hit it off right away but does she belong in his world?

<u>Lonely Billionaire Romance Series</u>

Tricia was hired to care for billionaire John's wife, who is dying. An unlikely romance emerges after his wife, Rebecca, gives John permission to pursue his happiness after she is gone.

<u>Ardent Billionaire Romance Series</u>

Deirdre doesn't know what to make of the gorgeous man that seems to be interested in her. His name is Parker Walters and he seems friendly enough. There is just something off about him. Why is he trying the hide the fact that he is the heir to his father's billion dollar software empire?

iii

<u>Fervent Billionaire BWWM Romance Series</u>

Alexandra had never been with a white man before. She had seen William at the café before but she always kept her distance. It was unfortunate that their first chance meeting happened when she dropped her breakfast and spilled coffee all over his expensive business suit.

<u>Audacious Billionaire BWWM Romance Series</u>

Chante is torn between staying close to a man beyond her league, and fleeing from him to spare herself from a hopeless position. But she finds she is propelled into a place where she needs to confront her doubts and cast her fate aside to follow the dictates of her heart. Damned if she does and miserable is she doesn't, how will Chante face the events that will lead her to a place of pure happiness or to the pits of a broken heart?

Get the latest update on new releases from the author at:

https://shylastarr.com/newsletter/

This book is Part Two of the "Tenacious Billionaire BWWM Romance Series"

Book 1 - Love Deceived

Adalia is too proud to accept help from the billionaire playboy, Trent Dawson. How long can she maintain her resolve? The bank is at her heels to repossess her business. To make matters worse, Adalia finds suspicious evidence of Trent's philandering ways. She must determine whether to trust Trent with the fate of her business and her heart.

Book 2 - Love Forgiven

Adalia is broken after a keen betrayal and the loss of her lifelong dream: her very own bakery. But she has to carry on, especially now that she's back living under her father's roof and has her semi-abusive ex-boyfriend's advances to contend with. She's determined to continue baking, even if she has to work at the local market for the rest of her days, but she can't shake thoughts of Trent and what happened between them.

Book 3 - Love Endured

Adalia Montclair is determined to be more than Mrs. Dawson. She's going to start her own catering business. But a surprise pregnancy throws a wrench in the works, in the form of her new husband himself. Trent is determined to keep Adalia safe, even if it means keeping her at home and away from her dreams, a fate she can't abide, even with a baby on board. Still, even with tension growing, Adalia can't keep her eyes or hands off her husband.

Book 4 - Love Everlasting

Adalia has just received the worst news of her entire
life. Her son, Isaac, is gravely ill, and the only way to
save him is a revolutionary treatment which will cost a
lot of money. But a lot of money is exactly what Trent
doesn't have, now that Space Inc. has gone under. Time
is running out and only by working together can Adalia
and Trent save their son. Their son's illness and
Michelle's interference threatens to tear them apart, but
Adalia isn't one to give up that easily.

Tenacious Billionaire BWWM Romance Series

Love Forgiven

Book Two

By Shyla Starr

Table of Contents

Chapter One

"**THEY WANT** them Black Forest cheesecakes done in thirty," Melanie said, chewing on a stick of gum.

Adalia sighed and blinked a couple times. "I'm not a miracle worker. Besides, I hardly think anyone in the store is going to riot if I don't get it out on time."

Annie's Market specialized in nothing but providing loads of baked goods to as many customers as possible – in short, the quality was terrible. The recipes in the bakery section were set and Adalia's creativity was stifled, but a job was a job and God knew she needed the money after that debauchery with Trent.

Melanie shuffled out of the kitchen and the doors swung in her wake. The girl had about as much finesse as a bull on steroids. She'd worked there for a week as Adalia's manager, and it was difficult to respect her.

Failure, failure, failure. The word repeated itself in her head.

Measure out the flour, *failure*, weigh the sugar, *failure*, beat the eggs, *failure*. It didn't matter what she did or which way she looked at things. She'd messed up. Big time.

Melanie shoved back into the kitchen. "Store manager says to get 'em done or you're in trouble."

"You went to the store manager?" Adalia stared at her and shook her head.

"Yeah, and there's some guy here to see you."

Adalia's heart leapt into her throat, and she stopped moving completely. Screw the Black Forest cakes, what if Trent had arrived? Mortification paralyzed her; she was glued to the spot.

The last thing she'd want was the billionaire to see her slumming it in a tiny store bakery.

"Who?" Adalia whispered.

Melanie raised an eyebrow. "Derick or something, I didn't hear proper. Get them cakes ready." She turned and charged out again, still chewing gum like it was her air to breathe.

"Derick," Adalia said to herself, shaking her head in confusion. Who the hell was Derick? She dusted off her hands on her grubby apron and strolled out of the kitchen and into the kiosk area.

It wasn't Derick; it was DeShawn.

"Hey baby," he murmured, resting his elbows on top of the glass case, and gazing into her eyes. "I've been thinking about you all day."

"I'm honored," she replied, and the sarcasm was lost on him. She didn't want to see Trent, but she surely didn't want to see her ex-boyfriend either. He'd pretty much messed with her mind for long enough, and she didn't need that added pressure or drama.

"You working here now?"

"No," she grumbled. "I just come here to work out."

"Huh?"

"Nothing," she said with a sweet smile. "What do you want, DeShawn? I've got things to do right now." She glanced out over the empty store and made eye contact with the manager.

He glared at her and tilted his head to the side like the oversized buzzard he was. "Hurry up," he mouthed then tapped his cheap Kmart watch.

She forced herself not to roll her eyes at the authority figure. Once upon a time, she'd loved baking, but that was when she'd been able to create something from fresh, not stick to the plan, no matter how disgusting it was.

"Baby?" DeShawn's voice interrupted her train of thought.

"What is it?" She snapped her focus back to his face. "Like I said, I'm busy."

"And I said I want you back."

Agony erupted in her chest, pushing aside every other emotion. She'd been through so much, tasted a hint of success and then fallen hard. All she wanted was to get back on her feet and move on with her life, but DeShawn was back.

"Why? Give me one good reason why."

"Because I love you, baby," he said, leaning over the case of day-old cakes to grab at her arm. She didn't jerk it away and he managed to bring it up and take hold of her hand instead. He brought the tips of her fingers to his lips and kissed them gently.

There wasn't heat like there was with Trent, but it still brought out something in her. Something good. A long forgotten memory of what it was like to be touched by a person who cared.

Did DeShawn truly care?

"I don't trust you, and I don't need that," she said, pulling her hand from his grasp and wiping the back on her apron with a sour expression.

"You never gave me a chance to prove myself to you. I love you so much, baby, and you ain't never given me the chance to show it."

"What are you talking about?" she spat, trembling from head to toe. "I gave you every chance in the world to show your love for me and you didn't make any effort whatsoever."

"I came to your daddy's place to talk to you."

"What?!" Adalia laughed out loud and the manager shot her a look of pure loathing. "I'm not talking about after I dumped your sorry ass. By then, it was too late.

I'm talking about before. Because when it really mattered, you didn't give a crap."

"I was high a lot of the time."

"Precisely." Adalia gripped the low-slung counter with both hands.

Melanie appeared beside her. "You gotta get back to work. The Black Forest cakes aren't gonna bake themselves."

"What the hell does a store need two managers for?" Adalia blurted, then snapped her mouth shut.

Melanie glared at her for a minute then charged off again, muttering to herself.

That meant more trouble for her. The bakery manager chewed and steamed her way over to the store manager and flung her arms around, describing what Adalia had said in minute detail, apparently.

"You realize how busy I am, right?" Adalia breathed slowly, through the anger and disappointment in herself.

"Yeah, true that. Look, girl, I can't live without you. I'm not gonna treat you bad again. Only give you what you deserve. You gotta believe me."

"No, DeShawn, all I 'gotta' do is work and keep this damn job so I can earn enough money to make rent this damn month."

"So, come live wit' me." DeShawn grinned and spread his arms wide, then scratched beneath the line of his do-rag. His muscles rippled beneath his tank top, but she didn't have that spark with him.

Maybe she'd never feel that chemistry again. Hell, she'd probably imagined it in the first place.

"I'm not moving in with you, DeShawn. There's no question about that in my mind."

"Aight," he said, then rapped his knuckles on the glass counter. "So lemme take you on a date."

The store manager held up a hand to Melanie's face, then walked past her and marched in Adalia's direction.

Some of the shelves in the store leaned skew, the cans had a layer of dust which matched the grime on the front windows. Hardly any sunlight made it through to the back, so the fluorescents buzzing and clicking overhead made perfect sense.

"You need to leave now," Adalia murmured, bracing herself for the complaints from the manager. "I ain't leaving," DeShawn said. The manager, Mr. Hubbard, was almost at the kiosk.

"What?"

"I ain't leaving until you say you'll go on a date with me."

"Do you realize I could lose my job over this? Do you even care?"

"I care about you, but I ain't gonna take no for no answer, and you need to see that, girl." DeShawn seemed oblivious to the risk he'd put her under just by showing up. She was at the end of her tether with him and with everything else.

Mr. Hubbard was steps away.

"Fine, I'll go on a date with you. Just get outta here!" She hissed it at him, then plastered up a broad smile.

"Adalia," Hubbard said, stopping beside DeShawn. "I'd like to see you in the kitchen for a moment."

"Yes, sir," she said, still with that sick, fake smile on her lips. It suited how she felt inside: nauseated by the situation and what she had to do each day. She was a sellout.

"On Friday, baby," DeShawn called out after.

The kitchen doors swung shut behind her.

Chapter Two

"Adalia, you're treading on thin ice here." Hubbard pointed his finger right under her nose and waggled it around, spreading the smell of baking cake through the kitchen. "I told you I wanted these Black Forest cakes ready and they're not, are they?"

"Mr. Hubbard, I apologize but –"

"Are they?" he repeated, frowning at her, daring her to give him lip. God, she wished she could, but she had to keep this crappy job.

"Not yet, sir."

"Then what are you doing chatting up customers in my shop?"

It wasn't technically his shop, it was Annie's, but he liked to strut around as if he owned the place. That was what sleeping with the boss got you. If you had no morals, of course.

"I wasn't chatting him up, sir. He paid me a surprise visit. I assure you, I had no intention of –"

Hubbard raised a palm to her face then clipped his fingers and thumb together to make a 'talking' motion. "Yeah, I'm hearing too much of this. You need to get back to work and get those cakes out of the damn oven. Don't let me hear you giving Melanie cheek again, either. She's above you, and you need to accept that."

Adalia glared at him for a minute, but softened her gaze slowly. She wouldn't stoop to this guy's level. He obviously had an inferiority complex – maybe he was bullied as a child or something, who knew?

"Yes sir, understood." She gave him a winning smile, and his frown deepened. "I'll get back to work."

Mr. Hubbard charged out of the kitchen and the doors swung shut behind him then rebounded again.

Melanie traipsed in with an expression of smug satisfaction on her mug. She chewed and chewed and chewed on that damn gum. "You talk to the big boss?"

"Yes," Adalia said, gritting her teeth and strolling to the ovens. She checked the timer, then switched it off and brought out the cakes, one-by-one. Melanie burned a hole in the back of her head as she worked, but she didn't turn around and talk to her.

"You think you're better than me or somethin'?" Melanie growled between lip smacks.

"Pardon?" Adalia tipped the cakes out onto cooling trays and went to wash her hands. She scrubbed them, running the water loud to block out the manager's inquiries.

"Hey," Melanie yelled over the rushing water from the faucet. "I asked if you think you're better than me."

Adalia sighed and turned to face the younger woman, who had dark brown hair and a lurid pink streak through the front of it. That was the fashion with teenagers nowadays, and Melanie couldn't be a day over nineteen.

Her mascara was badly smudged at the corners of her eyes, and had formed clumps in the middle of her eyelids.

Did Adalia think she was better than Melanie? No, she didn't think she was better than anyone, and that was the God honest truth. She was definitely a better baker than Melanie and that was what grated her the most.

"Answer my question or I'll go talk to Mr. Hubbard again."

The girl had to be insecure to take this much of an issue with a snappy comment.

"Honestly? No, I don't think I'm better than you, Melanie. I think everyone's equal and that's the difference between your view point and mine."

"What're you trying to say?" Melanie spat her gum into the trash can next to the door and pulled herself up to sit on the counter.

"Nothing that really matters anymore. Just that I have work to do, and I'm sure you do too." If that wasn't amicable in the face of severe irritation, then what was?

Melanie narrowed her eyes and mulled her words over for a few minutes, then gave up on figuring the sentiment out and gave a snort. "Whatever, just get them Black Forest cakes done, y'hear?"

"Sure," Adalia replied, "just waiting for them to cool."

The other woman slid off the counter and clomped out of the kitchen again. Peace and quiet at last. Adalia let out a relieved sigh and rested her forehead against the fridge to cool it.

There was too much pressure building and now she'd agreed to a date with DeShawn to top it all off. Friday night. Maybe she could dig her way to China by Friday night. Or somehow raise enough money to take a bus out of the city. Who was she kidding with that?

If she left, he'd damn well follow her. The guy was persistent.

Riiiiiiing.

Her phone tinkled to life in her pocket and she gave a beleaguered sigh. That had to be DeShawn, calling to confirm. She brought it out, clicking the green button without checking the ID.

"Yes? Now's not the time, as I'm sure you know." Adalia leaned against the steel fridge some more, bathing her nostrils in the scent of cooling cake.

"Adalia, it's so good to hear your voice again." It was Trent. Trent Dawson was on the phone with her.

Her heart raced for a moment, and she gripped the phone tight.

"What do you want?" she snapped. "What do you actually want this time, Trent?"

"Jesus, relax," he said, then chuckled. "I see you haven't changed in the past couple months."

"Oh, I've changed all right." She didn't elaborate on the point. He didn't need any information about her life, just like she didn't need any about his. She'd had more than enough of this.

"I wanted to talk to you about something serious, and I thought I'd call, since you probably wouldn't like it if I popped in for a visit."

Adalia glanced around at the kitchen and a cold sweat broke out on the back of her neck. She clicked her low slung heels on the linoleum and shaded her eyes from the fluorescents.

"You don't know where I am."

"I figured you'd be at your father's place. I looked up his address, but yeah, I didn't want to risk it."

"You realize I can just hang up on you anyway."

"Sure, but then you'd miss out on the opportunity I've got for you." Trent oozed confidence, but Adalia didn't buy it for a second. She knew him too well by now. His voice held a slight tremble, which meant he was nervous about this.

He didn't let on much weakness, but she was tuned into it now, to break past that alpha shell and to the truth beyond.

Adalia charged to the door and checked on Melanie through the window. The girl twirled her gum around her finger and chatted up a couple of teenage boys who'd entered the store. Mr. Hubbard stood in the background, fiddling on his smartphone.

"Adalia?"

"Get to the point, please."

"Right. I'd like you to cater a few functions for my company. We've got several events coming up, and I'd be happy to have you on the team for them."

Adalia laughed until tears gathered in the corners of her eyes.

"Excuse me?"

"You heard me. I want some more of those chocolate buns."

"How dare you say that to me?" Adalia slammed her fist onto the countertop then instantly regretted it. Melanie's attention flinched from the boys to the kitchen door and back again.

"What are you talking about? I'm offering you a great chance to get ahead here, maybe get back on track with your bakery idea."

"Trent, I don't need your damn help. You never got that! Not for as long as we knew each other, you just didn't understand that I don't need you." She'd lost control of the situation. He did that to her – it was some emotional manipulative gift he possessed that drove her over the edge every single time and she was sick of it.

"Adalia," he started.

"I'll tell you what, Trent. Why don't you ask Michelle Van Heerden to bake for your events, because I am not interested." She pulled the phone from her ear and hung up, then tossed it into her purse under the counter.

Adalia turned back to her cakes, heart as heavy as lead.

Chapter Three

A few days later, Adalia kicked off her shoes in the kitchen back at her dad's house. There were dishes piled in the sink and carrots lying on the chopping board. She scraped the peeler over their fat bodies and threw the peelings into the trash can.

She'd decided on a beef stew for the evening. She could put it on, leave it for her father and come back after her date for leftovers if she was still hungry.

Adalia checked the clock on the wall. She still had a couple hours before eight and DeShawn was usually late anyway.

"Hey, you're back from work." Her father, Sylvester, shuffled into the kitchen wrapped in his blanket. He coughed into his fist then sniffed. "I didn't think you'd be home this soon."

"I took a bit of time off work. Got a date tonight," she muttered, hoping he wouldn't pick up on that last detail.

"A date with who? That billionaire fella?" Of course he'd heard, just her luck. Once she let him in on this secret, she'd never hear the end of it.

"I'm making a beef stew for dinner, so you can just fetch yourself a bowl when you get hungry. Be sure to turn the gas off after a few hours. I've microwaved a bowl of rice to go with it. You got that, Dad?" Adalia chopped the carrots and plopped them into the stock and meat simmering on the stove.

"You don't want to tell me who you're going with." Sylvester Montclair was no fool, and he was grumpier than usual because he was sick.

"Dad, it's not a real date, actually, so what does it matter?"

"Girl, you know better than to keep secrets from me under my own roof," he grumbled then walked a few steps to the fridge, pulled it open and brought out a beer.

"No alcohol, Dad. It will weaken your immune system. There's a carton of orange juice in there. Have that instead." Adalia pointed with the wooden spoon and put on a 'cute daughter' smile.

"Don't tell me what to do in my house." He popped the cap and glugged back the brew. He really was terrible when he was ill. "Now, who are you going out with? And don't evade the question this time. It's starting to piss me off."

"DeShawn asked me out."

Sylvester slammed the beer bottle onto the wooden table. "Are you kidding me?"

"No, Dad. Look, it's not what you think. I didn't go after him, he came after me. He came right into work and –"

"So, not only is he harassing you, but he's disturbing you during work hours, too? And you're going with it. I thought I raised you better than this, girl." He snatched up the bottle and drank some more, eyes already glazing over from lack of food.

"Dad, I had no choice but to say yes at the time."

"Every time there's the slightest hint of trouble, you go running back to that character. He's useless and you know it. Still a drug addict."

"He's quit, he told me so a short while ago." Adalia stirred the pot and turned her back on her father. She didn't want him to see the tears.

"And you believed him, of course. You'd better get your act together, Adalia, because I will not permit that kid's presence under my roof."

Adalia gritted her teeth. "I won't bring him here." There was all this 'under my roof' shit ever since she'd had to move in. There was some unknown pressure building, and she had a feeling it was financial.

Her father had never been this hard on her before.

"You'd better not. Minute he steps over my threshold is the minute he gets a right hook to the jaw."

Sylvester wasn't a violent man either. None of this made any sense to her.

"I can look after myself," she murmured, though she wasn't that sure she believed it anymore.

"I'm beginning to doubt that, girl. I want you to make me proud, not afraid for your damn future."

"No pressure," she remarked, then tapped the wooden spoon on the side of the pot and rested it on a saucer beside the stove.

"You're damn right there's pressure on you. This is your life, and I don't want to see you screw it up like I did."

"What are you talking about, Dad? You have a great life. You've got a home, a job, a happy family."

He grumbled under his breath then spoke up. "I have what I have, but you're not focusing on creating something for yourself. Leave the men in your dust, girl, or you're going to regret it. Time will pass in a blur, and someday soon I'll be dead and you'll be old and gray."

"I've never heard you this negative before. It kinda scares me." Adalia folded her arms and studied the lines around his eyes and on his forehead. His shoulders were tense, and there was strain running through him.

"I'm disappointed in you on this one, Adalia. I thought you were smarter than this." He scuffed his feet along the tiles and made his way through the arch that led out into the living room.

"Thanks, Dad," she whispered under her breath. She lowered the heat on the stove, covered the pot with a lid, tilted it to let steam out then hurried to her room.

Hours passed and she took her time getting ready. She didn't do too much makeup, but chose a nice dress, not too formal. It was DeShawn after all. She didn't need to impress him. He'd be oblivious anyway.

She went out to check on the stew at a quarter to eight. The meat was tender but not quite ready and the aroma tempted her to drop the dinner date and stay home. There was nothing like a good stew to soothe an aching heart.

Aching for Trent, not DeShawn. She grimaced at herself. Why did it matter who she ached for? Why couldn't she just forget about him and focus on starting her life back up again?

Each morning it was the same… she'd wake up, think of Trent, go to work, more thinking of Trent, come home, Trent again. She couldn't take this anymore!

Adalia fished around in the stew and brought out a piece of potato. She blew on it until it was cool, salted it, then popped it in her mouth and savored the flavor.

The clock ticked over, past eight and to half past. She stared at it, shaking her head at herself. Her dad was right. She shouldn't have agreed to anything with DeShawn. She should've been stronger in the bakery, but at the moment, everything had seemed so extreme, so dire.

Now, she was stuck in her Friday night best, waiting on a man she didn't want to see in the first place.

"He's late," her father called from the living room, and her stomach tied up in knots.

"I know, but the stew will be ready in an hour, okay?" At least he'd had a massive lunch. Adalia pressed her hands to her sides and swallowed hard. She was too anxious about this – it was just DeShawn!

"Told you that he was no good."

"I know, Dad," she murmured, but he didn't reply. Adalia paced back and forth, glaring at the clock. She was humiliated and it transformed into anger. That red heat built within her, and she gave a low growl. The clock ticked onto nine, and she gritted her teeth.

Where did he get off? He'd asked her on this stupid date and –

There was a knock at the door. She squared her shoulders and charged through the living room, past her father and to the front door.

DeShawn was about to get it.

Adalia grasped the handle, pulled the door open and gasped.

"Wha – what are you doing here?"

Trent Dawson smiled back at her. "I had to come see you."

Chapter Four

"What do you want?" Adalia regained her composure as quickly as possible. It wasn't easy with him staring back at her. He had such a soulful gaze, and it pierced right through to her core.

Trent ruffled his blond hair and tilted his head forward to gaze at her from under his brow. He held a brown dossier in his right hand and rested the other on the doorjamb. "I've got a proposition for you."

"No," she said, immediately. "I'm not interested in your propositions, Trent."

"You should be. This could change your life for the better, for good." He tucked the brown folder under his arm. Trent wasn't a patient guy, and her denial probably ate at him to the core, but so what? That was his problem and not hers.

She hadn't asked for any of this.

"Who's this?" Sylvester appeared in the hall behind her and she swallowed again. Her dad wouldn't like this one bit. Not after he'd seen her so broken over Trent in the first place.

He moved in beside her and glared at the rich white guy. "Adalia, who is this?"

"Dad, this is Trent Dawson. He's an important business man," she replied, avoiding the issue. The street behind him was still empty, at least. DeShawn would cause nothing but trouble if he arrived now.

"Trent, Trent," Sylvester repeated, then clicked his fingers and pointed. "You're the billionaire, correct?"

"Yes, sir, that's correct." Trent extended his hand for a shake. "It's a pleasure to meet you, Mr. Montclair."

Sylvester didn't take the proffered greeting. Instead, he pursed his lips and looked at Adalia. "This is even more disappointing."

"Pardon?" Trent frowned and neither of them looked at him.

"Dad, I need some privacy. Would you mind giving it to me?"

"This is my house. If you want privacy, take this outside." He motioned to the street, and she drew her shoulders up. She didn't want to have this argument in front of Trent, but her father's attitude stank of late.

Everything he said made her feel worse for staying with him.

"Fine," she replied then walked out onto the porch. Trent's frown stayed in place, but he followed her. The front door slammed shut, removing the sliver of light from the hall. Sylvester didn't switch on the porch light for them, so Adalia went to the stairs and sat down.

"Are you okay?" Trent settled in next to her, but didn't slip his arm around her shoulder. Trent had boundaries and he knew how to respect hers because of that.

"I'm fine. I mean, I will be fine. It's not a big deal. Besides, what do you care?" Adalia crossed her legs and gazed out at the street. The street lights were out in places, and the kids had been called into their apartment buildings hours ago.

There was silence except for the distant howl of sirens. This wasn't the best area of town, but she'd grown up here. She knew these streets like the back of her hand, and Trent just didn't belong.

"You look beautiful," he said, and she tensed up. That need for him resurfaced, but she pushed at it until it sank back into nothingness. She had to remain in control of her emotions around him, or it would be the end of her willpower.

"Thanks," she replied, then shifted further away from him. He grazed her thigh with the dossier and she flinched.

"Are you going somewhere?"

Adalia kept her silence.

"Adalia?"

"What is it?"

"Are you going out?" There was jealousy in the question and she hesitated a moment longer. "Who are you going with?"

"I've got a date, and it's none of your business who with. My life has got nothing to do with you. I've told you that before, and I'll tell you again until you get the damn point." She slapped her thighs to brush off the imaginary dirt and rose. She gripped the banister to steady herself.

She was afloat in her mind, detached from it actually, and watching the events unfold. That was what anxiety did to her and she hated it. She didn't feel real, but rather a faded image of her own reality.

"Fine, that's fine. Adalia, I didn't come to discuss your personal life." Trent set his jaw, then brought out that file and laid it across his knees. "I came to discuss something more important than that."

"I'm not interested in catering for any events."

"I heard you." He said it simply, but it set her nerves jangling. What was in that file? What did he have planned for her? She couldn't deal with surprises.

"I really ought to go back inside and check on my dad. He's not feeling well at the moment." She turned but he rose and caught her arm. That touch sent sparks dancing across her skin.

Adalia tried to pull away but he held her tight. "Let go of me."

"I can't," he whispered, and her insides melted into a puddle.

"Why not? Why is it so difficult to accept that I don't need you or your help?"

Trent breathed slowly, chest rising and falling close enough for her to reach out and caress. "Because I need your help."

Adalia's eyes widened. "The famous Mr. Dawson, buckling under his own ego? This is something new."

"Don't be facetious," he replied, finally relinquishing his grip and taking a few steps back.

"I can't help it. You're normally independent and in control. I can't help but think this is some ploy to get into my pants again."

"You think an awful lot of yourself, Montclair." Trent rearranged that blond hair again, and she twitched toward him then stopped herself. She had to resist that urge for him or it would overrun her logic.

"Just tell me what you want so I can go inside. I'll hear you out, but I'm not making any promises."

"All right, that's fine." He handed her the folder and she took it, though it felt like she'd grabbed a viper.

She didn't open the file. "What's in it?"

"A contract."

"Not interested," she said, thrusting the dossier back at him, but he didn't take it.

"Hear me out before you make a decision, Adalia. Christ, you're so temperamental."

She pursed her lips and folded her arms across her breasts. "Continue."

"I bought a new space, not the same place as your old one, and I've got everything in it to start a bakery."

"Right," she said, "and you think I'm going to work for you?"

"I'd like that, yeah. I didn't plan this around you. I just think the bakery idea is great and could make a lot of money if you, uh, I did it the right way." He nodded with self-assurance and she crumbled a little. She wanted to believe that he wasn't doing this just for her as some sick way of getting her into his bed again.

"Why don't you ask Van Heerden to bake for you, huh?"

"What is it with you and that? You know she's as bright as a fused light bulb and she certainly can't bake worth a damn."

Adalia's jealousy reared its ugly head. "And you know this from experience, I assume? A lot of home cooked meals gone wrong? A lot of dates."

"No," he replied, patient though his jaw was clenched so tight his muscle twitched in his cheek.

"I'm not interested in this. I'm not interested in working for you or being around you, and I feel I've made it amply clear."

"Adalia," he said, then paused and looked up at the waxing moon that peered out from behind the clouds. The stars were shrouded in patches, and those that twinkled were dimmed by puffs of clouds.

"I've got to go. I'll see you around." She strolled back to the front door, and he rushed up behind her. He grabbed her by the shoulders, spun her on the spot and pressed her up against the door.

A cool sweat broke out on the back of her neck in response to the pressure of his touch.

She was trapped in desire again, and she couldn't fight her way out. He was hard for her… she could feel it through his tailored pants and the fabric of her dress.

"Trent, you can't do this to me… you can't put me in this kind of situation." It was almost a plea and she bit her lip, then tasted blood and stopped.

He lowered his nose to her throat and sighed. "I understand." He stepped back and disappointment shattered her arousal.

"I need you. Just realize that. I need you to make this business idea work."

"All right."

Footsteps sounded on the drive.

Chapter Five

Adalia glared down the pathway at DeShawn. Of course, he would pick this moment to arrive. Trouble brewing.

Trent gave a low chuckle. "I see. So this is your mystery date."

"I'll think about your proposition, but I'm not making any promises." Adalia held the brown dossier to her chest, but Trent didn't make eye contact. His gaze was fixed on DeShawn, who had stopped midway on the path to them. He flexed his biceps beneath a cotton shirt and grinned.

"What you doing here, pretty boy?" DeShawn strolled up to them, hands out of his pockets but not balled into fists. That was a relief. She didn't have patience for an all-out brawl on her father's front lawn.

"That's none of your business, kid." Trent stretched his neck until it made a crack.

"Trent, I think we're done talking." Adalia opened the front door and met her father's gaze. He stood in the hallway with that blanket wrapped around his shoulders and a bowl of stew in his grip.

"You going?" He asked it with such vehemence that she blinked a couple times. There was too much pressure from all sides, and she didn't know how much more of this she could take.

"Yeah, I'll be back later. Have a good night, Dad."

"I can't say I expect you will," he replied, indicating to the men on the porch. Adalia swept up her handbag from the front hall table and slipped the dossier inside. She closed the door, shutting off Sylvester's head-shaking glare.

"I'm ready," she announced, but neither of the men looked at her.

"I can't believe you're going out with this jerkoff after all he's done to you," Trent said.

DeShawn hopped up the stairs. He rammed into Trent's chest, but the billionaire didn't budge an inch.

"Stop it right now," she hissed. "I won't have you fighting on my father's front porch."

They ignored her.

"You should be scared." DeShawn and Trent were nose-to-nose, breathing heavily.

"I've never been less afraid in my life."

"That's dumb, 'cos I know how much you like yo face and I'ma fuck it up."

"Stop it," she said, grabbing at DeShawn. She tugged at him but he didn't move away. It was like pulling a rock out of a mountain – it just wouldn't happen. "This isn't the time for idiocy. We've got a date, DeShawn."

"He doesn't care about that, Adalia," said Trent. "He only cares about himself. The sooner you realize that, the sooner you can get rid of this fucking poser."

"You better watch yo mouth." DeShawn pressed his forehead into Trent's. "C'mon, pretty boy, let's do dis. I been waiting months fo this shit."

"Are you crazy?!" Adalia whispered. "This is my father's house! My *father's* house and you want to fight in front of it. Get off the front porch. Now!"

Trent didn't move.

DeShawn didn't move.

To do that probably meant weakness in man language. Adalia glanced back at the front window, and the curtain twitched as if someone had been there a second before.

"You think she really wants you? She's so much better than what you deserve," Trent growled.

"She sure don't want you or else why would she go on a date with me?" DeShawn replied.

"This is not the time for a dick sizing contest," Adalia cried, and both of them perked up and snapped apart at the word 'dick'. "You're acting like children."

"It's 'cos I love you, Dalie." DeShawn gave her a doe-eyed look and she didn't slap him. She wanted to, though. This was absolute madness.

"You don't love anyone but yourself," Trent barked. The two men pressed against each other again.

"Trent," she said, "please leave… right now."

He swiveled and stared at her, jaw dropping slightly. "Are you kidding?"

"No, of course not. I've agreed to consider your proposition, but other than that, I have no interest in having you as a part of my life."

Trent stood there a moment longer, muscles tensed, bulging from the sheer power he had on hold, and then he broke away from DeShawn. He walked down the front stairs and down the path without saying goodbye.

His shoulders were taut, his head held high, but she could feel the disappointment in him. His gait was labored, and he unlocked his Bentley, climbed in and sped off a moment later. The hum of the engine disappeared a few streets down, drowned out by the whoop of an ambulance.

That was a nightly occurrence in the neighborhood, but Adalia hated the noise. She associated it with death and unhappiness.

"You okay, baby?" DeShawn leaned his lower back against the banister and peered at her through the dark.

"I'm fine. You're late."

"I'm sorry," he said, words slurring ever so slightly – God, he'd better not be high again – then continued, "I got caught up at work."

"Work?" Since when did he have a job?

"Yeah, I'm sorry I'm late, girl, but the biz come first."

Adalia nodded slowly, though fear had taken a hold of her gut. Work and DeShawn didn't mix well.

"So this Trent dude," he began.

She cut him off by raising her palm. "I don't want to talk about him. Let's just go on this damn date and get it over and done with."

"That don't sound good. Don't sound like you wanna go out wit' me." DeShawn folded his arms and took a defensive stance.

"At what point did I say I wanted to go anywhere with you? You forced me into this, DeShawn. You got what you wanted, so let's get on with this before I change my mind." She straightened her dress and slung her handbag over her shoulder. That dossier burned a hole in her brain.

He'd bought a bakery and he wanted her to work in it. What the hell did the document say? She could barely wait to get the date over so she could rush home, open it and kill the mystery.

DeShawn walked up to her and grabbed her by the chin. He squeezed hard and tilted her face upward to his. He brought his lips down and kissed her, taking from her what she wasn't willing to give him or anyone else.

She punched him in the gut, and he wheezed hard and backed off.

"Don't do that ever again."

"I'm sorry, Dalie. Wait. I can't resist touchin' you. I can't help it, girl." DeShawn gripped his belly and stretched his hand toward her. "I need you to come with me. Please," he begged and her heart melted a little. A tiny bit.

"All right," she agreed. She had to be crazy to allow this. Maybe her dad was right, but she wanted to get back at Trent on some level and this was her opportunity. "But you don't touch me like that again."

"I won't." He straightened then breathed slowly. "But I got a question for you, Dalie."

"And what's that?" She frowned. DeShawn was a man of few words and even fewer questions. Knowledge wasn't his 'thing'.

"You in love with this Trent guy?"

Her pulse raced, and she pressed her lips together. The sky had filled with clouds, and the shape of the moon was barely visible through the gray shroud. The stars were blocked from her view completely.

"I have nothing to say on the matter."

"So you do," he said.

Adalia marched down the stairs and started on her father's front path. "You coming?"

She couldn't truthfully answer that question without admitting it to herself.

And that she wouldn't do.

Chapter Six

Mike Montclair's office was decorated in mahogany and maroon. It was calm and regal, and it suited Adalia's brother's personality to a tee.

"It's wonderful to see you, Sis," Mike rumbled in those dulcet tones, letting her in with a bob of his head. He indicated the leather chair in front of his desk, and she walked over to it and took a seat.

"It's good to see you, too, Mike. I'm sorry I came on such short notice, but I've got a bit of an emergency." She plopped the dossier on his vast desk and rearranged his name plate. He was a partner in a law firm.

She'd never get over that. Her brother was a total success story, like something out of those semi-condescending Hollywood movies about black kids who grew up bad but ended well.

Their three brothers had died in turf wars or OD'd on drugs, but not Mike. He'd stuck to the books, worked hard and kept to his goals. He was her role model.

Her father was great, though grumpier than usual, but Mike was the real man to her. He'd never accepted handouts, paid off his own student loan and gotten to where he was through blood, sweat and tears.

He circled the desk and took up his chair, then folded his hands in front of himself. "How's Dad?"

Adalia raised her eyebrows.

"That bad, huh?"

"God knows I love him, but he's driving me up the wall. I don't want to sound ungrateful, but I could use a break from being in the house. He's as strict as he was when we were growing up, but it's worse this time around."

"Worse?" Mike frowned, and crinkles appeared at the corners of his hazel eyes.

"Yeah, he's not happy at all, and he doesn't seem happy with me either. He's got the flu, though, so that might be it."

"Maybe I ought to pay you guys a visit, check in and smooth over the rough edges." Mike had always had a way with Dad. They were best friends, and Sylvester respected his son for what he'd accomplished. But Mike had been neglecting his visits lately due to his busy work schedule.

A part of her wanted to resent the fact that Mike was the favorite, but she loved her brother too much to let petty shit like that get in the way of their relationship.

"If you want to visit, you can. It would be nice and I'm sure it would cheer him up, but Dad is the least of my issues at the moment."

"Right," Mike answered, nodding slowly and giving her an expression of sympathy. "I heard about the bakery. I wish you'd come to me about it. I might have been able to help you sort it out."

"You know how I am about this stuff, Mike."

"Stubborn." He chuckled and she picked up an eraser from his stationary holder and chucked it at his head. He caught it deftly then tucked it back where it belonged. "Seriously, you need to loosen up with that kind of thing. Rome wasn't built in a day and it surely wasn't built by one man, either."

"Yeah, but there was an emperor," she quipped and he rolled his eyes.

"I assume you didn't come here for a chat about Dad. What's the problem?" He settled back in his armchair and tilted his head to one side. It was the same action he'd used since they were kids.

She'd lost her favorite teddy bear when she was ten and he'd cocked his head to the side like that, looked at her and politely asked if she didn't think she was too old to have a teddy bear in the first place.

He was the rational kid on the block.

There was a knock at the door and a young, attractive assistant bustled in. "Good day, Mr.

Montclair, here are your messages," she said, wiggling her hips and handing him the notes.

Mike was oblivious. He accepted them then waved her to the door. "Thanks, Mel. Please make sure there are no further interruptions for the next hour or so."

"I won't take that much of your time," Adalia said, and the assistant shot her a look of pure jealousy. She snapped the door shut behind her. Mike was blessed with good looks and a football player's physique, so it was no small wonder every woman fell at his feet.

But he never seemed to notice.

"Take a look at this," she said then slid the dossier over to him. He flipped it open, took out the document and read it through once.

"Interesting," he said with a head tilt. "Care to elaborate on this?"

"Trent Dawson is –"

"Oh, I know who he is. Major billionaire involved in several charity organizations and a space pioneer to boot. But why did he buy a bakery? It doesn't seem like a fitting business endeavor for him."

"That's what I thought." Adalia crossed her legs, resigned to the fact that Trent wasn't interested in a business with her, but rather, in getting into her business.

"Explain," Mike said, spreading his hands wide.

"Trent and I are familiar with each other."

He raised a hand. "I don't want to know the details. I think I get the idea."

"Right. Well, Trent offered me a bakery a short while after I lost mine. He bought the same property and offered to let me run it as his silent partner. I said no for personal reasons."

"I understand. Hmm," Mike paused and cleared his throat, then studied the contract before him again, "I've brushed up on my contract law, so I should be able to provide you with some useful insight on this."

"Please do," she said, polite as could be. Mike did have a knack for drawing things out. He liked to dissect, rework, dissect again, and then assemble it all into one piece and discuss it for hours at a time.

"He's not offering to be a silent partner this time around, that much is clear."

"Then what is he offering? I couldn't make out anything from that legal jargon. The only thing I recognized was my name, his and the space for the dates and signatures."

"He wants to work with you. A proper partnership, fifty-fifty."

"What?! How would that even work when I have no financial backing?"

Mike hummed and stroked the desk, considering his words carefully, no doubt. "Simply put, he'd bring the money in and you'd be in charge of baking and running the business."

"But that's the same as a silent partner," she said.

"No, because it clearly stipulates here," he answered, pointing to a line of text on the page, "that he'll be working with you in the bakery itself in charge of marketing. It's under one of the clauses."

"That's ridiculous," Adalia replied, trembling in her chair. Could he really want this? There was no other reason for him to want it, other than to be close to her. That meant he was into the whole 'conquest' thing again.

How disappointing.

"He's attached a business plan, too. Hold on a sec…" Mike opened up the business plan and rifled through it. Adalia tapped her knees, waiting patiently. She hadn't even gone through that business plan. She hadn't wanted to give the concept a chance to enter her brain.

There was no room for hope.

"Yeah, he wants to work as the front man, with you baking in the back."

"You've got to be kidding me. What does he stand to gain out of this?"

Mike laughed and slid the business plan back into place. He carefully positioned the contract on top of it, then closed the dossier and gave it back to her.

"What does any business stand to gain? Profit. Revenue."

"Are you saying this is a legitimate contract?"

"Yes, it is most definitely a legitimate contract and proposition." He leaned back in his chair and studied her.

"But that doesn't mean I should sign. I mean, this is too weird."

Mike Montclair rested his arms on the armrests and gave her a knowing smile. "Adalia, you should go for it."

Chapter Seven

Adalia stood in the vast kitchen and stared at the clock on the wall. Trent usually came in at around nine in the morning and it was five minutes until then.

They'd been working together for a week now and she'd done her best to avoid him, but he'd made it increasingly difficult.

He came into the kitchen and talked to her when she was in the middle of a task. He discussed business with her. He laughed and joked around with the other kitchen staff, all the while shooting her the 'look'.

It was incredibly difficult to resist that look. The same expression she'd witnessed the night they'd made love for the first time. That deep desire for her, slathered across his face like sunscreen.

"You okay?" Jenny stood nearby, rolling out some pastry for an apple crumble.

"I'm fine, fine. Glad to have you on board." Her concession had been that she chose who worked in her kitchen. He'd agreed and had chosen the staff for the front only.

So far, business had streamed in and they'd been stacked with orders. It excited her, but it made her jealous at the same time. If only she'd managed to make her bakery work this way.

"I'm so glad that you're back doing what you love. I heard you were at one of the markets a short while ago, but I didn't want to pop in and visit."

Adalia reached over and squeezed Jenny's shoulder. "Thank you." She'd have been mortified if her old employee had witnessed her in a position like that. She'd never had as much fun quitting a job in her entire life.

The kitchen was alive with activity. Bakers hurried back and forth, creating treats and cakes. The aromas made her mouth water, but she was too preoccupied to even snatch a bit of icing or a taste of apple filling.

"Big orders today again, we'd better be on our toes." Adalia walked over to the oven and made sure it was at the right temperature. "Looks like we'll be catering for weddings soon."

"That's fantastic news," Jenny replied, wiping her forehead with the back of her arm and smearing flour across it.

"I think so," Trent said, strolling into the kitchen. "Though I've yet to discuss it with you, Adalia."

"When were you planning on it?" She punctured him with the question, poured every ounce of confidence into her being and stared at him head on.

"Right about now, actually." Trent indicated the office door nearby, but Adalia shook her head.

"There's too much to do for me to stop now." She took out a massive batch of cookie dough to illustrate her point.

Jenny coughed into her elbow and moved her pastry further down the bench, avoiding their conversation.

Trent opened and closed his mouth several times, then laughed. "That's fine, we can discuss it here. In fact, do you need some help with anything? We've got customers streaming in already. The cashiers can barely keep up."

"Trust me, I'm well aware," Adalia said, elbow deep in dough. "Grab me that tray."

He circled around the bench and got it for her, then plonked it on the counter. He brushed past her, pressing himself against her ass and she drew in a sharp breath. There was too much history between them, but there was also too much heat.

"You don't want to discuss the catering, now?"

"I —"

"Because we can always discuss it over dinner, if you'd feel more comfortable."

"No, that's all right, we can discuss it now," she said as quickly as she could. She took out the cookie cutter, and rued the fact that she hadn't insisted on an automated one. She plopped a big helping of the dough onto the counter and grabbed a rolling pin.

"I've got plenty of compliments on the quality of our products." Trent brushed off his suit and smiled at her. "I'm proud of the team we've got back here, you included."

"Thanks. Though it's mostly them more than it is me." She gestured to the other staff. There were people mixing, baking, rolling, kneading and it was a sight she'd dreamed of when she'd started out.

"We both know that's not true. You're at the helm and I'm proud of you, Adalia."

"Thanks," she repeated, and heat climbed up her neck and into her cheeks. "I'm really focused on making the quality outdo the quantity, though. I don't know how that fits in with catering for weddings."

"We'll increase the size of the team when it comes to that. Maybe build another team to deal with the catering side while you run the kitchen. Or you could run the catering side."

"Hire more staff?" She shook her head. "That's your solution to everything, isn't it?

"What are you talking about?" Trent leaned in, conspiratorial, another excuse to get in close.

"When there's a problem, you don't work through it. You just throw some more money at it until it goes away."

Trent straightened. "I throw money, focus, attention, hard work and everything else at it. It's called business, Adalia."

"That was a low blow," she retorted.

His eyes widened. "I didn't mean it like that."

"Whatever, we'll discuss this later. I'm busy now." She turned her back on him. There was pressure against it a second later, and his hot breath feathered across the skin of her neck.

Jenny's eyes widened and she hurried off, yelling orders to the other workers. Everyone else continued with their usual duties, ignoring the spectacle of Trent pressed up against her.

"I suggest you make your way over to the office, now," he murmured into her ear and goose bumps ran down her neck and spine. She pushed her ass into him, unable to resist and he grunted his surprise.

"Fine," she replied then slid out of his reach. "But let's make this a quick chat, because I've got work to do."

"After you," he said, gesturing to the office. Its windows had blinds, and there was plenty of room for privacy, but she still hesitated. "What are you afraid of?"

That spurred her on. She wasn't scared of anything, let alone a talk with Trent Dawson.

"Nothing." Adalia marched toward the office, opened the door and went over to the chair behind the desk. She sat down at her leisure, then crossed her legs and waited. The door closed shut behind her, and her pulse quickened. The blinds slid down to cover the windows and her heart beat a mile a minute.

"Finally, a minute alone with you." He stood beside her chair, but she didn't shift her gaze from the other side of the office.

"You going to sit down so we can talk?"

"Only if you sit on my lap."

"What?!"

Trent burst out laughing and circled to the other chair, then settled into it. "I'm kidding, of course, but you're sure fun to toy with."

"Yeah, you would know."

"What's that supposed to mean?" His brow wrinkled, but she didn't take it back.

"You've played me for a while, Trent, I'm used to your tricks. If you think you're going to get into my pants under the ruse of talking catering, then you are sorely mistaken, my friend." She rapped her knuckles on the desk. There was an image of the Golden Gate Bridge hanging on the wall, one Trent had taken on a business trip.

Her certification was on the opposite wall, and the potted plant in the corner gave the office a serene atmosphere. It was ruined by the sweltering heat between them.

Adalia was aroused in spite of her words. The thought, the mere hint, of doing anything with him in the office while everyone else was out there carrying on with work as usual drove her wild.

"I've never gone out of my way to hurt you. I've done the opposite in fact," he said, then smacked his lips. "But I won't lie, I still want you. I still think of you every night."

"Trent, don't say that, I can't handle it."

He rose and came around to her again, then dropped down on his knees in front of her.

"I want to taste you."

Chapter Eight

Bang!

The door slammed open, and Trent flinched back from Adalia's knees. She swiveled in the chair. Her heart sank then was set ablaze with burning hatred.

Michelle Van Heerden stood in the doorway, staring at them with her hands on her well-shaped hips. Thin and comely at the same time. She was the perfect woman with her long, blonde hair and her plush 'blowjob' lips.

"What are you doing here?" Adalia snapped out each word with so much force that Michelle shuffled back an inch.

She strode in a moment later, flashing a confident smile. "I came to find Mr. Dawson."

Trent rose to his feet. "You're a warning away from getting fired, Michelle. I've had enough of your interruptions."

"Sir, I had an important call from Mr. Harrington regarding a business endeavor."

Trent quirked his left eyebrow. "That is surprising. I didn't think I'd hear from him again." He glanced down at Adalia but she refused to be humiliated.

Sure, she'd walked in naked and argued with Trent in front of old Harrington, but she wouldn't apologize for it. He'd broken her heart and destroyed her trust. It was only fitting that she did something drastic.

Besides, she'd only wanted to confront him.

"Yes, he's most interested in pursuing a deal with you, in spite of citing personal reasons for his last drop in communications." She pointedly stared at Adalia, who wasn't about to take this crap from her. She stood and slid in close to Trent's side.

Their hips touched and that electricity sparked, mingling with her irritation at Michelle's appearance in their office. It was *their* office, Adalia's as well, not *just* Trent's, which meant she had as much say over what happened in it.

"I'm going to have to ask you to leave, Ms. Van Heerden. We're in the middle of a meeting."

"Yeah, that looked like a real serious meeting, Ms. Montclair," Michelle said with a sweet tone in her voice, but the intent was clear.

"Michelle, watch what you say. I'm not going to warn you about insubordination again. I've given you plenty of chances and I'm running short on patience now," Trent said.

"Finally," Adalia whispered to herself and only Trent heard. He pinched her lightly on the ass and she gave a low yelp, a mixture of shock and desire.

Michelle unbuttoned the top button of her V-neck cotton shirt. It plunged, revealing her cleavage and a thrill of jealousy passed over Adalia. Why did her main 'competition' with Trent have to be a fucking playmate?

Van Heerden's grin widened – as if she'd heard Adalia's thoughts – and she purred out another sentence. "As you wish, Mr. Dawson. I didn't think I'd interrupt anything when I came in here, I apologize."

"Apology accepted," Trent replied, then went around to the other side of the desk again, releasing the need Adalia had for him. Time slowed and she breathed in the fading scent of his cologne.

"Yes, I assumed Ms. Montclair would be in the bakery where she belonged."

"Where I belong? I'm co-owner of this establishment. This is my office as much as it is Trent's."

Trent opened his mouth and she made a swift chopping motion with her hand to silence him.

"And what do you mean 'where I belong'?"

"Oh, no offense meant, I simply meant you're the head baker or chef or whatever it's called, so I figured that was where you'd be."

Adalia narrowed her eyes then swept invisible dust off the surface of the table.

"And of course, the position suits you so well." Michelle said, with a vindictive smile.

She met Michelle's gaze again, but didn't ask the question on the edge of her lips. *What do you mean?*

Van Heerden continued, one hand still on the door handle, the kitchen bustling behind her, "I mean, at least I think it does. I'm not sure how many of the cakes actually make it out to the customers."

"What the fuck does that mean?"

"That you clearly eat a good portion of them before they get out there. Don't get me wrong, there's no shame in tasting to see if it's right, but eating that many cakes can't be good for business." Michelle pointed with her manicured fingernail, indicating up and down Adalia's length.

"Shut up," Trent said, in an even tone. "Don't you ever speak to Adalia like that again. Do you understand me?"

"Sir, I didn't mean –"

"Do you understand me?"

"Yes, I understand. But I think it's outrageous that you're taking her side over mine when we've been in business together for years and –"

"The only reason you have this position is because your father was friends with my father. Don't kid yourself that I need you in this firm. You are on your last leg, Van Heerden, and you can bet I will have no problem phoning your father and telling him just how badly you've been behaving of late."

Michelle went the color of the walls, whiter than white, then turned a vague shade of green. "That won't be necessary."

"I think it will be necessary. You've overstepped your boundaries too many times," Trent said, bending over some papers on the desk, nonchalant, unconcerned by Michelle's reaction to his words.

It was the best business practice Adalia had seen. If only she had a pen and pad to take notes – Trent was masterful with this stuff. And a lot of other… stuff.

"I'm sorry, Mr. Dawson," Michelle hissed, raising her shoulders. She buttoned that shirt up again and didn't look at Adalia. Her cheeks reddened under scrutiny.

"You don't sound very sorry." Trent clicked on the mouse beside the computer and settled into the chair. "You sound like you're asking for me to give your dad a call."

"Please don't. I'm sorry for my behavior, Mr. Dawson." Michelle softened her tone to a near-whisper, but Adalia didn't buy it for a second. She wasn't sorry at all. Man, what she'd give to get this chick on her own and give her a serious talking to.

"I'm not the one you have to apologize to," Trent said, finally raising his gaze to meet his assistant's. She gave a tiny shake of her head, in denial or disbelief, her eyes flickering to meet Adalia's then back again. "Express your remorse to Adalia for your actions."

"Trent –"

"Now."

Michelle's entire body gave an almighty twitch. She stared at Adalia, scorching her with pure hatred. "I'm sorry."

"Good. Now get out of this office and tell Mr. Harrington I'll call him back in an hour."

"Yes, sir," she replied then turned on her heel and fled. She slammed the office door in her wake.

"God, it's like dealing with a teenager," he said.

"Thanks for that, but I could have handled it." Adalia was stiff and the sentence matched her body. She didn't need emotional or financial charity from him, but she'd loved seeing him take Michelle down a peg.

Trent went over to the plant and examined it. "Did you know this is fake?"

"No, I didn't, but what does it matter?"

"Plants are good for breathing. Good aesthetic." He came over to her and slipped his arms around her waist.

"But then, what better aesthetic than to have you in the room, Ms. Montclair."

"I don't feel like being played today, Trent," she replied, trying and failing to wriggle away from him.

"I never play games, Adalia. You should know that by now. I was so sure I made myself clear with you."

She shuddered against him, taken in by the smell of his skin and the intensity of that stare. There was no question about it… if she kissed him, she'd fall under his spell again. She'd lose her strength and sanity… she'd let him take her on the desk.

Her mouth went dry.

"Yes," she said, "you've always been clear with me."

"Good." Trent brought his mouth to hers, but she slipped her index finger onto his lips and pressed him away.

"You've been very clear. You're a player and I promise you, Dawson, I don't have time for your games."

Adalia went back to the bakery, throbbing for him.

Chapter Nine

Adalia held the credit card bill in the light, so she could read it properly. Her heart sank, but she couldn't look away from the figures at the bottom of the page. Her dad was in debt and there was nothing she could do about it but find another place to live.

"Dad?" she called out, softly in case he was actually asleep. "Dad, are you up?" It wasn't that late, but he'd been ill lately.

"I'm in the living room," he grunted and she made her way through and sat down opposite him. He was laid up on the sofa, covered in a blanket. He'd sniffled less at breakfast, which was surely a good sign he'd be back on his feet soon. Not that he hadn't paid his dues already, but a business didn't run itself, certainly not one of the plumbing variety.

"Can I talk to you for a sec?"

"Thought that's what you were doing, girl," he grumbled, and muted the TV. It was some high speed chase down the highway, and his attention remained glued on the screen, despite the lack of sound.

"I found this." She held up the bill and he glanced at it and then back at the TV.

"Shouldn't go rifling through someone else's mail, Adalia. It's rude."

"I thought it was for me." She was so used to living alone that when she saw the surname Montclair on the letter, she assumed it was for her. "I only realized after I'd read it that it was yours."

"Yeah, yeah," he said, "what do you want to know, girl?"

"Dad, are you in trouble financially?"

"The bill should have made it plain that I am." He still didn't give her his full attention.

"What's the matter? Is the business not pulling in enough money?"

Sylvester heaved a sigh then pushed himself upright at an angle, to better rest his back on the arm of the cream sofa. "It's difficult to pull in money when you're not working due to illness."

He hated being idle, she got that, but did he have to be so curt with her? She was just trying to help.

"What happened to Fred?" He was the assistant at the shop, and usually went out to do the heavy-duty jobs that Sylvester couldn't handle.

"Had to let him go."

"Why?!" Adalia kicked off her high heels and tucked her feet underneath her butt, retaining the alarmed posture she'd held since the start of the conversation.

"Because he relocated to another town. Haven't had a chance to hire anyone else 'cos I've been ill, and it doesn't look like I'll be able to afford it at this rate."

"Dad, everything's going to be all right." But guilt plagued her. She'd moved in shortly after he'd kicked out his last tenant. Her father usually stayed in the basement, the old room Mike had lived in before he'd left home, and rented the main floors out to a family or a bachelor or anyone willing to live in the shitty neighborhood.

With her in the house, that source of revenue had dropped, too.

"Dad, I'll move out." Adalia dropped the credit card bill on the wooden coffee table.

"What are you talking about? Who said anything about moving out?" Sylvester made an impatient clicking noise with his tongue. "You always jump to the worst conclusions, my girl."

"I wasn't born yesterday, I know you were renting this place out before I came along and that I've kinda cut down that source of revenue. Look, the bakery's doing really well, I can afford it."

It was a lie. This was the first month of the new business, and they were on Trent's financial backing. She'd get a payout but it wouldn't be huge until they were fully established.

"You're staying," he said, then unmuted the TV as if that was the end of the discussion.

Adalia talked over the blaring sirens and crazed commentary. "I'm going."

He muted it again and turned to her. "I like having the top floor to myself, I like having you in the house. I don't feel so damn lonely anymore, and I'll be on my feet in no time. You're staying in this house."

"Dad, come on, we both know that's not true," she said in her most patient tones, but it seemed to set him on edge anyway. He straightened up further and swung his legs over the side of the sofa. "You're still sick and you haven't improved enough to get back to work. The doctor would freak out if he knew you'd even suggested it."

"It's a common cold, it will pass."

"Yeah, but not for a while. No offense, but you're old and these things take time. It would be much cheaper for me to move out now, rather than leech off your resources for another month."

"Adalia, I do not want you to leave this house until you can afford it. Can you?"

She swallowed hard. She couldn't lie to a direct question like that. Adalia Montclair was many things, and a terrible liar was definitely on that list.

"That's what I thought. There's no use trying to hide from it, girl. We need each other right now and I don't want to see you move out before I'm sure you're back on your feet good and proper."

"What about you? You're not exactly a spring chicken. Should you really be running around, fiddling with toilets all day long?" She couldn't help getting irritated about this. She hated that level of control her father had over her, but he was right and she couldn't change that.

"I am what I am and I'll do what I need to do to survive. Besides, if I'm ever in any real trouble, Mike will help me out." Sylvester didn't realize he'd pitted her brother against her again, but Adalia was used to it.

He slid down on the sofa again and reached for the remote. "We done here?"

"Yeah, I guess so. Is there anything you need?"

"Cup of coffee would be good. No, wait, a cup of tea. No, wait, a cup of coffee."

"Hot cocoa?"

"That's the stuff," he replied, then tapped the side of his nose and pointed at her. "You've got a gift, my girl, for knowing what people need and when." He unmuted the TV and went back to his viewing pleasure.

Adalia stood and strolled into the kitchen, but her emotions were anything but easy. She was most definitely a financial burden to her father. She'd bought groceries where she could, tried to pay her way, but the money she'd earned at the market had barely covered it, and she'd yet to see any return from the new business endeavor.

There had to be a way she could get out of there and fast.

If her father got in trouble with banks, he'd have nowhere to go except to Mike, and God knew he needed his independence.

Adalia gritted her teeth and boiled the kettle, then went to get milk out of the fridge. There was a car backfire outside, or a gunshot, and she jumped slightly, sloshing some of the fluid onto the floor.

"How's that cocoa coming?" Sylvester yelled from the living room. "It's getting interesting in here. You wouldn't want to miss it."

"I'll be right there," she called back, but she wiped tears from her cheeks after she'd answered. There wasn't enough milk for the cocoa, now.

Adalia fetched the tea instead then put the bag into her father's old, chipped mug with a sigh.

She wouldn't ask Trent for money. She simply wouldn't. She just had to find another way of getting out of her father's hair, so that he could get back on track.

The title *Adalia the Burden* didn't suit her.

She shrugged her shoulders and poured the boiling water into the mug.

Chapter Ten

"You could stay with me," Jenny offered, "if you don't mind the live-in boyfriend and sleeping on the couch."

"I wouldn't do that to you," Adalia said, unlocking the front door of the bakery. It was early in the morning, so early that the birds hadn't even started chirping yet. That was how it went in the trade, bake early, sell fresh.

"Come on, it wouldn't be a big deal."

"You and I both know that wouldn't work, Jen. I appreciate it, but it just wouldn't pan out." They filed in, the first to arrive and she closed the door behind them and flicked on the lights in the shop area.

It was decorated in candy blues, pinks and pearly whites. There were cute cupcake signs and places for people to sit. Hell, there was even a coffee bar. Trent had an eye for what worked, and this definitely worked.

"Why not?" Jenny dumped her bag on the counter and popped a hip. She whipped out her chef's whites and pulled them on over her tank top, then proceeded to button them up.

"Because I'd get on your nerves and end up staying longer than I should somehow. Actually, no," Adalia said, then followed Jenny's example, "it's not that I don't have a plan. Look, I'm going to get paid something at the end of this month, it's inevitable, but it's the lead up that worries me."

"Your dad's in that much trouble?"

Adalia's voice cracked slightly. "I'm afraid another month might break him. It's getting urgent now. I had no idea that things were that bad for him financially. Seeing the bills was an eye opener."

"Then come stay with me," Jenny urged, bustling over to her. She squeezed Adalia's arm and peered into her eyes. "It will be fine, I promise. A friend in need and all that."

"I'm not anyone's burden. I refuse to be. Besides, he wouldn't let me go if he knew it's in with a friend and not to my own place. He's weird like that."

"He just wants what's best for you," Jenny replied then turned her arm squeeze into a pat.

"Yeah, well we'd better get to baking before the sun rises." Adalia turned toward the kitchen and they walked in together.

The silence of the kitchen lulled her. She loved this feeling.

Deathly quiet followed by the slow hum of the machines, the focus of working on dough with hands. They never spoke during this time. From the minute they entered the kitchen until the sun rose, the only sounds in the kitchen were the bangs and clangs of trays, and the soft poof or squelch of dough being teased into shape.

It was the pure time. Hours of total peace without interruption. This was how life was meant to be and how the day was meant to start. No yoga or exercise, instead, the peace of the craft.

Slam!

The front door of the bakery opened and shut, and they met each other's gazes. What was that about? The other employees were never this noisy when they came in.

Adalia was loathe to break the silence, and Jenny kept her mouth shut, too. Their hands were covered in flour, and Adalia's fingers were sticky with dough in between.

"'Lo? Dalie?"

Jenny's frown was punctuated by a raised eyebrow. It probably sounded like a foreign language, but Adalia was too familiar with it by now.

"What do you want, DeShawn?" She marched to the sink and washed her hands, then scrubbed them on a paper towel. Their date had hardly been worth mentioning.

DeShawn stumbled into the kitchen then braced himself against the doorjamb. "Where you at, woman?"

"Have you gone blind? Or has the alcohol rendered you dumb?" Adalia turned and waved at him, then rolled her eyes. "I don't have time for this now, DeShawn. I've got work to do."

"You said you gonna call and you never did."

"Just because I said it, doesn't make it true." She gritted her teeth. She hadn't meant to lie to him. She'd purely forgotten the minute he'd dropped her off at home. That night she'd gone over the contents of the dossier and sent her brother a text to organize an appointment.

"How drunk are you right now?" She examined him from afar with her fists on her hips. "Because this barging into places seems to be a trend with you."

The front door of the bakery opened and closed again. The other workers entered the kitchen, filing past with the rising sun, chattering but giving DeShawn a wide berth. The scent of alcohol wafted through the room and a few of them rubbed at their noses.

"Jenny, organize them please. I've got a personal matter to attend to," she said, pointing to the others in the room. Then she walked up to DeShawn and grabbed him by the wrist.

"Baby, I had to –"

"Don't speak until I get you out into the front of the shop."

She frog marched him through, and he miraculously obeyed the command. Adalia positioned him in one of the chairs and paced up and down in front of him.

"I hesitated about giving you another chance at a date with me because of this kind of behavior, DeShawn."

"I'm not that drunk," he said, then gave a low burp and didn't bother stifling it behind his hand.

"And I'm not that stupid." Adalia breathed deep to calm herself. She couldn't believe she still had a smidgen of remorse for this guy. Hell, she still had feelings for him, even after their past.

"I don't got that much dough, don't got no fancy car, but, girl, I'll look after you if you let me."

"I don't need you to look after me. I need a partner who's strong, who cares, who respects me for who I am."

"I need you in my life, baby, you are a rock to me."

"So we've gone from you protecting me to me supporting you. That's exactly right, though. All I ever was to you was a means of support. Someone to lean on in tough times."

"That ain't true."

Adalia sighed and looked around the bakery. She'd arrived where she'd wanted to, kind of, and she couldn't go back into the past. It wasn't right. It wouldn't solve any of her problems.

"How's your old man?" DeShawn slurred and she flinched. He'd picked up on that? No, it wasn't possible, he'd come in after they'd finished talking about it.

"He's fine." She folded her arms.

"Word is he struggling."

Adalia's heart beat faster. "Where did you hear that?"

"People talk." DeShawn rubbed his eyes then rested his hand on his chin, but his elbow slipped off the table and he jerked upright.

"Well, people are wrong a lot of the time." She dropped her hands to her sides and clenched her fists instead.

"Whatever, baby. If you needs a place to stay, I got your back."

"Thanks, but no thanks," she replied. "DeShawn, you'd better leave."

"What?! Ah, c'mon, girl, I come all the way out here to see you," he grunted, and struggled to his feet. "At least lemme take you on another date."

"No, DeShawn, you were late for the last one and you're drunk right now. I don't want to date you. I don't want this kind of drama in my life."

"I'll quit drinking," he announced, then stumbled to one side and regained his balance.

"Yeah, and the sun will stop shining tomorrow." Adalia shook her head. No matter how she felt about him, she couldn't let it overcome her common sense.

"Okay, just give me one last chance to prove myself."

"No, you've had plenty of chances."

"Don't be such a bitch," he snapped.

She gestured to the door. She didn't have time to respond to idiocy. She would call him once he'd sobered up, and they could discuss his behavior.

"I'll call you, DeShawn. We can talk about this because it's obvious you're not going to stop this madness."

"Madness? I ain't mad." DeShawn's drunken rage grew and he straightened his spine, glaring at her.

"Get out now," she said, and the door of the bakery opened.

Trent stood there, early for once, glaring at DeShawn. "What do we have here?"

Chapter Eleven

Adalia walked backward until she hit the counter, then leaned against it and breathed through her nose. Sunlight had only just begun to shine through the front windows, and the warm scent of baked bread filtered through to her soul; a form of comfort at its finest that took her back to times past.

But none of it made any difference to Trent and DeShawn.

Her drunk ex-boyfriend – could she really call him that when she'd been on date with him recently? – clambered out of the chair, knocked it over, then shoved it back with the heel of his sneaker.

"He giving you trouble?" Trent asked, gesturing lazily. He had on a stylish suit, but without a tie and his shirt was unbuttoned at the collar. His hair was styled to perfection, and his muscles strained against the tailored jacket.

DeShawn was the opposite.

"No, everything is under control, thanks," she said, dusting her hands off. There was too much tension in this room, and she wanted out. More importantly, she wanted DeShawn out before there was a problem.

"You think you better than me or somethin'?" DeShawn cracked his knuckles. His white wife-beater was stained with sweat under the arms.

"Adalia says you're leaving," Trent answered, then unbuttoned his jacket and stripped it off. He tossed it onto the counter and it slid off the other side of the glass surface. "So leave."

DeShawn raised his chin. "You leave."

"This is my shop, I'm not going anywhere." Trent interlocked his fingers and stretched them outward, as if limbering up for a fight.

"I'm so tired of telling you two not to fight. I don't have time for this insanity." Adalia snatched up Trent's jacket and tossed it at his chest, but it hit and flopped to the floor in a heap.

Trent stepped over it, oblivious to her anger. Maybe he didn't care how she felt anymore.

"I'll call the cops if you don't get out of here." He reached into his pocket and drew out a smartphone, then tapped on the screen. He still seemed at his leisure, like he was calm as could be.

"You ain't gonna scare me off this time," Deshawn said, shambling forward on unsteady feet. The temperature in the front end of the bakery was moderate, not hot enough to bake cookies or anything, and it wasn't as if there was a heater on, but sweat poured down DeShawn's arms, his biceps were pulled taut. He lifted his fist and examined it, smiling. His front tooth was chipped – that was new – and he reminded Adalia of a chipmunk for a second. Funny enough as it was, she didn't find the comparison amusing.

"That's enough, both of you." Adalia strode between them and put her palms up to separate the men. "I don't care what you do outside of the bakery, but we're going to have customers streaming in soon."

Trent and DeShawn moved as one, Trent left and her ex-boyfriend right. They stayed in sync and inched toward each other, acting as if she didn't exist. This whole issue was because of her, but they pretended her opinion didn't matter when it came to their little 'man feud'.

"This won't end well for you. I don't even have to call the cops to get rid of you. Do you know that?" Trent's smile was forced, his teeth were clenched.

"Bring it on." DeShawn pounded his left palm with his fist.

The men collided with each other, chests touching, nose-to-nose. DeShawn's sneakers squeaked on the tiles, shifting under the pressure they exerted on each other.

The golden bell above the door tinkled, and a young woman with two children strolled in, one about ten and the other, who had to be four, clutched a Hello Kitty doll to her chest. The mother held their hands and tossed her braids over her shoulder, yellow, green and red beads clattering at the ends. She walked a few steps, then stopped dead in her tracks and glared at DeShawn and Trent.

"Uh," she murmured. She hesitated for a moment and the little girl's eyes widened. The mother tugged her kids toward the exit.

"Wait, please, take a seat," Adalia said, but the woman didn't pause. She gave the men a backward glance then disappeared through the door, which clanged closed behind her.

That was it.

"Hey!" Adalia yelled. The two guys hadn't popped apart at the sight of a customer. Instead, they circled slowly, bumping chests every now and again and muttering curses at each other. "Hey, we just lost a customer because of this damn shit." Adalia slapped the nearest table and it wobbled.

"Get the fuck out of my shop," Trent growled, rolling up his sleeves.

"I ain't leavin' 'til Adalia leaves wit' me." DeShawn shoved Trent in the chest and the billionaire stumbled back a pace. DeShawn took the momentary weakness as his drunken chance.

He rushed at Trent, trailing whiskey fumes, and tackled him around the middle. Trent exhaled an 'oof' and flew backward. He hit the front window of the shop and it shattered.

The men fell over the rim and into the street.

Adalia slapped her hands to her ears. She was frozen in utter shock. A gaping hole had replaced the window where their frosted cupcake sign had been painted. She swallowed back a wave of tears, but the fury that went with them stayed. In fact, it got worse.

She charged out of the front door, crunching glass beneath her pumps. The men rolled in the street, and Trent was on top of DeShawn. A cut trickled blood down his forehead, and it dropped onto her ex-boyfriend's bare shoulder, mingling with the rancid sweat.

"Get off him," Adalia shrieked. And she wasn't sure who she meant.

"You're going to pay for that," Trent grunted, then pulled his fist back to knock DeShawn on the jaw.

"Stop it," Adalia yelled and he glanced up at her. There was so much anger in his eyes, but it faded quickly. He shook his head as if waking from a deep sleep, or a nightmare for that matter.

"Adalia, I'm so –"

Crack!

Trent's head snapped back and he keeled over, fumbling at his jaw. DeShawn's fist was in the air – he'd punched up when the billionaire hadn't been looking. His knuckles were cracked and bleeding, but his expression was pure delight.

"What have you done!?" She gasped and hurried to Trent's side. She knelt next to him, ignoring the gathering of folk on the pavement, and the glass stabbing at her knees. "Talk to me, Trent. Are you okay?"

His eyes rolled, but they stayed open and dazed. DeShawn scuffled to his feet, glanced left and right. Police sirens rang out in the distance. He turned and took off down the street, then disappeared around the corner.

"Stay with me, Trent. Everything will be fine." It was a knock to the jaw. *He couldn't have a concussion, surely.* "Trent?"

"Get away from me," he murmured, clarity reappearing in his gaze.

"It's me, it's Adalia."

"I know. I told you to get away from me. Now." He placed his palms on the concrete then pushed himself into the sitting position. He stared directly ahead, at a spot on the wall of a brick building opposite, at the candy-striped barber's pole attached to it.

"I'm so sorry. I didn't think he would come here." Adalia grimaced at herself. He'd picked a fight with her ex so why was she sorry? Why was she the one who always had to compromise?

"Is nothing sacred?" he asked quietly then brushed his fingertips over his jaw, probing the injury.

"What do you mean?"

"He's in your home, he's at your dad's place, he comes to our bakery. Nothing is sacred from that guy, and it's because you allow it." Trent knuckled his forehead.

"I didn't invite him into my life," she answered, then rose to look down on the top of his head.

He continued staring into space, not meeting her gaze. Apparently, there was nothing more to say.

Chapter Twelve

"Your knees are bleeding," Sylvester said, around a forkful of macaroni and cheese.

Adalia glanced down at the drying blood and didn't say a word.

"You want to tell me what happened, girl?" her father asked, dropping his fork into his plate and scooching up on the couch. He was in the living room again, with that blanket draped around his shoulders and a TV dinner clutched between his wrinkled hands.

The illness had aged him over a matter of weeks, and it set off an ache in Adalia's chest. There was too much guilt to bear. She'd failed her business, her father, and now Trent. Hell, she'd even failed DeShawn on some level, though that seemed a bit of a stretch.

"Adalia," her father barked, and she straightened. She dropped her fork and pushed the tray away onto the coffee table. The TV was on mute for once, and there were no high speed chases blaring in the silence. Only a news reporter.

There'd been a shooting in the neighborhood and an unarmed innocent person was hurt. Anger gripped her, and she gestured to the set to distract Sylvester.

"Yeah, that's been running all day. But I'm more concerned about how you injured yourself, right now." He stabbed a macaroni tube and waved it at her on the end of his fork.

"There was an accident at the shop."

"An accident?" He grunted, then popped the macaroni into his mouth and chewed noisily. "What kind of accident?"

"The kind that breaks glass, Dad, it's not important." Adalia picked up her tray again and wrestled her macaroni around with her fork.

"You're not telling me something." Sylvester leaned back and studied her over his empty plate. "There's no point keeping it inside, Adalia. You need to talk and I'm here for you."

"Here for me? Dad, you're hardly 'here' for yourself. How can I possibly ask you to support me when you've got enough trouble as it is?" She grabbed his empty tray and took it to the kitchen with her full one.

"Everything is fine," he grumbled from the living room, but she didn't go back in. Sylvester Montclair was determined to refuse her help, financially, emotionally and in any other way, yet he put pressure on her to open up.

It was ridiculous.

The doorbell rang, and she swore under her breath. She wasn't in the mood for DeShawn. Adalia stomped off down the hall, then straightened her blouse and opened the door.

"Hi," Trent said, standing with his hands tucked behind his back, chest pushed out. Purpling bruises ran up the side of his jaw and his cheek, but he didn't seem bothered.

"What are you doing here?" she asked, gripping the doorjamb. Trent had been furious after the fight. She'd expected him to avoid her, maybe even tell her that she wasn't welcome in his bakery anymore. He'd gone on so much about it being 'his shop'.

"May I come inside?" He didn't move, simply waited, the picture of patience, the complete opposite from the afternoon.

Adalia didn't reply, but stepped back from the door. He entered, and his footsteps resounded on the wooden floor. She glanced out into the empty street, illuminated by flickering neon light.

Trent brought his hands to the front and swung them at his sides for a moment, then frowned and held them still. "I don't agree with what happened today."

"I said I was sorry. Look, I didn't invite DeShawn there. I told him to leave even before you came in," she murmured, brushing a bit of macaroni off her skirt. "But then again, you did fight him. You didn't have to do that."

"There are only so many times I can put up with a certain type of behavior before I snap." He unbuttoned his jacket and left it hanging open. He dressed casually… at least it was casual for him, with a tight white shirt, jacket and jeans that clung to his thighs.

"I know DeShawn can be irritating, but –"

"I'm not talking about DeShawn's behavior." Trent silenced her without motion. The words were more than enough.

"What? My behavior?" Adalia's attitude soured instantly. "What the hell are you talking about?"

"You continue to allow that man back into your space. You know his presence in your life is detrimental, yet you allow it," Trent replied, his speech business-like, clipped off. He kept his distance. The heat between them was non-existent.

"I don't allow anything. I can't control him," she insisted, poking her palm with her fingernail. The jabs of pain kept her grounded.

"Clearly. That or you don't want him out of your life." Trent sneered.

"Stop it. I don't want DeShawn interfering. I've asked him multiple times to butt out, but he won't listen. Like I said, I can't control him." Adalia walked through to the kitchen and took out two coffee mugs. He followed, but she didn't watch him. She didn't want him to see how happy she was that he was in the house. The way she felt about him made Adalia feel pathetic. Why was it like this? This was worse than a crush, or even love… it was an addiction.

She clicked the switch on the coffee maker and it bubbled to life.

"You making coffee, girl?" her father called from the living room.

"Yes, I'll bring some in for you in a moment." She took out an extra mug, and Trent pressed against her back, then ran his hands up her arms and rested them on her shoulders, with his thumbs at the base of her neck.

"I have a proposition for you," he whispered, nuzzling her neck with the tip of his nose.

"Now is definitely not the time to proposition me, if you know what I mean," she answered, jerking her head in the direction of the living room.

Trent chuckled then nipped her neck, sending shivers down her spine. "That's not what I meant."

Adalia frowned and brought the sugar out, then placed the bowl on the counter and turned to him. He didn't back off right away, but lingered in her space, consuming her gaze with his.

"What do you mean proposition? I'm still in the middle of your last proposition and that's only led to a broken window." She braced her palms on the counter.

Trent stepped away. "I don't like the thought of DeShawn coming by here and causing trouble for you and your father."

"That's really none of your business."

His laugh was throaty, like an old-time villain from a movie where the woman gets tied to the train tracks. "You're my partner. Of course it's my business."

Adalia spooned sugar into the mugs. "What's the proposition?"

"I want you to move into one of my apartments. Rent won't be much and you can stay there without a deposit or paying anything until the bakery takes off." Trent spread his arms and shrugged. "What do you say?"

Adalia dropped the spoon into a cup and blinked, staring at the backyard. This could be her answer to everything. She could get out of her father's house, help him save money on groceries, and get rid of DeShawn all at once.

But it was too much. What if he wanted something in return for the favor? And this was kind of like a handout.

"I know what you're thinking, but this isn't charity. I'll expect you to pay the deposit and first month's rent back to me, once we get the ball, or should I say croissant, rolling at the bakery." Trent was dead serious.

She spun on the spot to answer him then froze. Sylvester Montclair was in the doorway, blanket gone and back straight. He glared at Trent, who met his gaze without blinking.

"Absolutely not," her father growled. "You're not living with this guy."

"Dad, it's not like that, and anyway, this isn't your decision to make." Adalia strode forward, but Sylvester held out a hand to her.

"Not my decision. Hah, guess you're right about that, girl. It's not like you owe me anything." And with that, he disappeared into the living room.

Chapter Thirteen

There weren't that many boxes, but Adalia loaded them in the hallway anyway. Sylvester didn't help, but stood in the doorway, with one shoulder leaned against it and an expression of disdain coloring his features.

"I don't approve of this and I never will," he grumbled, as she shoved another box out of her bedroom and into the entrance hall. "You're making the biggest mistake of your life."

"Dad, I'm well past worrying about that. I need to do what's best for me right now, and what's best for you, too." Adalia hurried back to her bedroom and lifted a box of her favorite books, romance and crime fiction mostly, then carted it out. She dumped it just when it got heavy, then sat down on top of it and crossed her ankles.

She stared at her father. He was too old, gray eyebrows, wrinkles and all the accoutrements that went with it. Certainly too old to continue with the business by himself.

"Have you considered what this could mean for your future? This man clearly wants one thing from you." Her dad didn't have the blanket on, and his cough had wheezed away on its own over the past few days.

"Yes, I've considered that, and I don't have a choice right now."

"Of course you do. Stay here with me like you have all along." That was close to a plea from him. Adalia quirked her eyebrows at him, but he didn't back down. "What, you don't like living with your old man? Is that it?"

"No, that's not it. Tell you what," she said, tapping her chin with a finger, "I'll stay if you'll let me pay the rent and buy more groceries."

"No, that's not necessary." The answer was immediate, and his jaw was set with stubborn resolve. The same kind she'd inherited from him. He wouldn't budge on this point, that much was plain.

"Then I won't be staying here. You don't need the extra financial strain. It's as simple as that."

The doorbell rang and she stood, dusting off her hands. Butterflies jittered around in her stomach, reverse transformed into caterpillars and squirmed all over the inside of her rib cage, then swapped back to butterflies.

Trent was here to pick her up. Hopefully, her father wouldn't give him too much stick, but judging by his demeanor that was too much to hope for.

Adalia unlocked the door and swung it open, then blinked a couple times. DeShawn stared back at her, sober and with a shirt on for a change. There was a green 'M' on the front, and his jeans were spotless.

"Hey, baby, I had to come see you to apologize for –" He noticed the boxes and a frown creased his dark forehead. The do-rag was off and his hair was in braids, like the night they'd first met.

"Now's not a good time," she said, and her father snorted out loud.

"What's going on here?" DeShawn stroked his cheeks then swaggered inside. He lifted a hand to her father in greeting. "How you doing, man?"

"Much worse now that you're here, boy. What the hell do you want?" Sylvester's sweater was as wrinkled as his cheeks, and there was a spaghetti sauce stain on his checked shirt, like a blood stain.

"I came to talk to Dalie." DeShawn gestured with his thumb. She checked the street and breathed a sigh of relief. Trent wasn't in sight. That meant she still had some time to get rid of her ex before Trent turned up with a truck or a Cadillac or a goddamn helicopter, knowing him.

"Like I said, now really isn't a good time, DeShawn." Adalia held the door open for him, but he didn't move toward it.

He kicked one of the boxes with his booted foot and her books toppled inside. "You going somewhere?"

Adalia rushed over and checked that there wasn't any damage. "Watch it with these!"

"Where you going, Dalie?" DeShawn's frown stayed put.

She patted her box of books then rose from her crouch with a soft sigh. She'd have to deal with him, because some part of her, whichever part, owed him that much at least.

"Dad—," she said. Sylvester huffed before she could finish her sentence and walked off in the direction of the living room. The TV blared to life a few moments later, on a cartoon this time. He had a penchant for Daffy Duck.

"DeShawn, I've told you time and time again that it's over between us and that I'm moving on."

"Yeah, and I told you I ain't givin' up. You mine, girl." He grinned, and the mixture of joy and the constant crinkling of his forehead disconcerted her.

"I'm not yours." She folded her arms under her breasts and he openly admired them for a moment. "Hey, snap out of it. I'm not yours, DeShawn."

"Then why you go out wit' me?" He paused, ran a hand over his forehead and felt the wrinkles. "Wait, why all yo shit packed up?"

"Because I'm moving out," she said, finally. Better to rip the Band-aid off now. The street was still empty of her business partner, so she stepped up to the door and shut it halfway.

"Moving out?" He kicked the box again and she hissed at him, but he ignored it and continued, "Where you going?"

"I'm moving into an apartment." Adalia considered the situation then nodded to herself, firmly. "I'm moving into one of Trent's apartments."

DeShawn's shoulders came up fast and air whistled out of his nose. "What the fuck for?"

"Because he offered me a place and I took it."

"So you take it from him but you don't wanna live with me," DeShawn stated. His voice echoed in the hallway and she guarded her boxes, just in case. She dropped down on top of them, utterly exhausted.

"I've told you I am not interested in being with you so many damn times I've actually lost count. You have no say over what happens in my life." Adalia formed each word with calculated care, firing them at him so he would finally understand she meant business.

"Bitch, you don't get it." DeShawn didn't shout, he whispered it, and fear crawled into her heart.

"Don't call me a bitch."

"Well, you actin' like one. You don't get it. I love you. I wanna be wit' you, and you trippin', runnin' around actin' like you better than me." DeShawn crouched down in front of her then stared deep into her eyes. "You think you better than me, but you go out wit' me when I ask. You ain't nothin' but a ho."

"Get out of my face," she muttered, pushing him by his shoulders. He didn't fall, merely rocked back for a second then regained his balance.

"You ain't worth a damn, but you's mine. You should feel lucky or some shit, that I care enough to haul yo ass out of trouble." He gripped Adalia's arm, fingers biting into the flesh.

"Let go of me," she said, ripping from his grasp and rising quickly to hop back over the boxes and into the doorway.

The TV in the living room carried on, Daffy Duck spluttered, "That's despicable."

"Get the fuck out of here, right now." Adalia pointed to the exit, and DeShawn moved toward her. A car horn honked outside and he stopped then hurried out onto the porch – maybe he thought it was Trent too.

But it wasn't. A school bus rattled down the road. DeShawn turned to walk back inside and she slammed the door shut in his face, then triple locked it.

"You can't hide from me, Dalie. You can't hide from me forever."

Heavy footsteps stomped away, but she didn't open up until Trent called to her from the other side of the door.

Chapter Fourteen

Trent dumped the last of her boxes onto the sofa and put his fists on his hips. Adalia stood beside him, staring around at the small, but well-furnished apartment. This was better than what she'd had before.

"What do you think?" he asked. She walked through to the kitchen and stroked the cool steel of the fridge door.

"It's lovely," she whispered, but her heart wasn't in it. DeShawn had always been too intense. He'd been overly interested in her from the start then as soon as he'd had her the attention had dropped off. But this? This obsessive need and continuous interference?

It set her nerves tingling in the worst ways.

What if he actually hurt her? What if he hurt Trent?

"There's something on your mind," Trent said, appearing in the kitchen.

She nodded and went to the sink, then swept a glass from the drying rack and filled it with water. She drank it down in a few deep gulps.

"Talk to me, Adalia. You know you can trust me," he said, but he didn't close the distance between them, which was kind of a relief. She didn't need their heat as an added distraction. There were layers upon layers of guilt now.

"I don't want to talk," she said.

"I know you do," Trent insisted.

Adalia couldn't handle it. Too much pressure from too many sides, and the pressure cooker's lid popped off with a bang.

"You don't know anything about me," she screamed, then dropped the glass into the sink. It shattered against the metal bottom. "You want to believe you know what's best but you don't know anything."

Trent didn't react.

"I don't need this kind of pressure from you," she continued, gaining speed. "I don't need your pity and your pep talks. I just need to be alone."

"I won't leave you to deal with this on your own. I want to help you." Trent's voice was a soothing balm, and her tears came on hot and fast. He walked over to her and wrapped his arms around her waist, then tugged her tight against his body.

Adalia soaked in his rugged scent, lowering her head to meet the crook of his neck. He smelled fresh and his skin was toned. He stroked her hair then ran his thumb and ring finger down either side of her spine and she arched her back.

"It was DeShawn," she murmured, lips touching his skin.

Trent's hand slowed and he shrank back to look into her eyes. "What did he do?"

"It's not what he did, it's how he acted," Adalia replied.

"Did he hurt you? Threaten you?"

"Kind of, I don't know. He's just claiming me like I'm his property. I can't get rid of him and I'm afraid he'll find me here." She ran her hands up his arms, then rested them on those biceps, which were balls of tension.

"No," Trent answered, and flexed involuntarily. "He won't find you and I'll deal with him if he comes near the bakery again."

"But what about my dad?"

"Your dad will be fine. I'm pretty sure DeShawn won't go there now that you're gone." Trent nodded. That assurance in himself and his ability to handle the situation gave her a major confidence boost, and she needed it after a few months of uncertainty.

"Thank you," she whispered. She was malleable now. She'd given up on so much of who she was, the stubbornness had been stripped bare, but a tiny voice inside her whispered that she was better than this.

She knew she was better than DeShawn and felt ashamed for not standing up for herself. She shouldn't need a man to watch her back.

"And as for property, or territory or whatever. Adalia," he said, then brushed her cheek with his rough knuckles, "you're nobody's property. But you are the woman of my dreams."

She drew in a shuddering gasp. "You don't mean that."

"Of course I do," he replied, then brought his lips to her throat and trailed a line of hot kisses down to the curve of her cleavage. He unbuttoned her blouse slowly, and sweet desire flooded her middle and sped through her limbs.

"Trent, I'm afraid," she murmured, and he paused with a finger hooked into the cup of her lacy white bra.

"I'll protect you, I swear it." He dragged the fabric down and sucked her nipple, circling it with his tongue.

Adalia ran her fingers through his hair and jerked his head back. Trent snarled and glared up at her, animal desire rippled through his torso and arms. He gripped her breast, and she pulled his hair, bringing him to his feet.

"But who will protect me from you?" Adalia asked.

"Can't help you there," he grunted, then crashed into her, parting her lips and kissing her until her toes curled. He lifted her with ease and she wrapped her legs around his waist, clinging to him.

Trent walked from the kitchen, kissing her neck, mouth, then along her jaw and back to her mouth again. His hands traveled everywhere, caressing and grabbing, like he couldn't get enough.

The bedroom wasn't far and he banged the door open with his foot and carried her in backward, so she wouldn't get the brunt of the impact. He was desperate to get her onto the bed, and she was grateful. Her juices had soaked through her thong, and she shifted, rubbing against him to relieve herself a little.

"Adalia, you naughty girl," he whispered, and she giggled. He dumped her onto the bed then stripped off his belt and pants in one go. They dropped to his ankles, and he stepped over them and tore her skirt upward, so it was a belt over her stomach.

He inserted a thumb under the strap of her thong then tore it off and tossed it into the corner. It'd been too long and they needed each other too bad. No time for foreplay. She clapped her legs around his waist again and he fell onto the bed, arms strong on either side of her head.

He pushed his throbbing dick inside her and they cried out together. She slid her arms around his neck and they kissed again, both trembling.

"Trent," she whispered, but he silenced her with another kiss. He plunged into her with satisfied grunts, abdomen tense from focus. He threw his head back then met her gaze and she moved with him, angling herself upward so he could penetrate her fully.

"I love you," he murmured into her mouth, and suddenly it wasn't so much desire for him as it was the need to be a part of him. There was nothing but the moment and their movement.

He slowed down, and she savored every thrust with a low moan.

"I love you," she murmured, and he kissed her tenderly, saying her name softly, over and over again, whispering it on her skin.

He turned her onto her stomach then entered her again, groaning, and she arched her back and pressed her ass into him. "Don't do that, you'll make me come," he commanded.

"That's what I want. All of you inside me. I want your cum inside me," she said, in breathless gasps, and she pushed into him more, bending so that he could admire the curve of her hips and back.

"You're so gorgeous," he grunted, and then he pounded into her. Pleasure coursed through her, pulsing and growing until she couldn't take it anymore.

Adalia came hard, clenching around him and gripping the floral pillow as an anchor. He followed her, squirting deep inside, and rocking her through the final throes of her own climax with his growl of release.

Trent didn't roll away, but slipped his arms around her chest and dragged her closer, then nuzzled her neck. He didn't pull out of her.

"I really do love you," he said, and warmth stroked her heart, awakening her to the truth of those words. He did love her, he did want her, and she felt the same way.

Adalia snuggled into his arms and he squeezed her once before soft sleep took her into a dream that wasn't half as sweet as their reality.

Chapter Fifteen

This had to be the answer. This was the only way to get rid of DeShawn once and for all, even if it hurt him. Adalia massaged her chest and stared up at his building, heart pounding against her ribs.

She was never this nervous. Not for DeShawn, certainly, he'd lost his chance with her ages ago, so why did she feel so… hollow? Adalia reached into the glove box of her tiny car, a loaner from Trent, and took out a bag of peppermints. She ripped it open and the candy erupted out and sprayed all over the passenger seat.

"God dammit," she grumbled, then snatched one up and crunched it between her teeth. The mint sweetness flooded her mouth and she breathed the stinging flavor through her nostrils. DeShawn's apartment was on the third floor of the brick-faced building. The exterior was cracked and faded, a trash can expelled its guts over the concrete and a group of kids, teenagers actually, loitered on the corner.

There was an exchange of cash and three of the teens wandered off down the road, acting casual, their jeans hanging below their butts, exposing their boxers. The other guy, who they'd left behind, lit a cigarette and leaned back with his foot cocked up against the bricks.

Drug dealer. This was her father's neighborhood, her deceased brothers'. Hell, it had been her neighborhood as a kid, but she still couldn't get used to the sight of drugs and money changing hands.

Adalia shivered and shrugged on her coat, though she wasn't that cold. The trembling was from anxiety. She steeled herself, squared her shoulders and got out of the car, then slammed the door closed and locked it.

She walked a few paces, turned back and jiggled the door handle, just in case. The drug dealer perked up, tipped his cap back with a finger and gave her a grin – his grill was gold and speckled with small diamonds.

Adalia hurried past him and up the concrete steps then barged through the broken wooden door. The buzzers on the wall were obsolete and the entire mechanism hung askew. She swallowed and headed for the elevator, then stopped at the 'out of order' sign.

Yet another obstacle, albeit a small one.

Adalia took the stairs in measured steps, stalling constantly. A woman with a cigarette between her lips and curlers in her hair charged into the hallway, closely followed by a shirtless guy covered in tattoos. Their argument echoed down the spiral staircase, but she continued up.

The rancid scent of sweat and stale smoke permeated her senses, and she coughed to clear her lungs.

DeShawn's door was cracked open, which meant he was in. That was his 'thing', his way of proving that he didn't have to worry about anyone hurting him because he was too scary to fuck with.

That had been a major issue for her when they'd dated.

Adalia pushed the door open and it creaked inward.

"Aw yeah, baby, that's so good." DeShawn's voice traveled between the scarred sofa and ashtrays filled with discarded butts. "Don't stop, girl."

She knew that tone, she'd suffered through it for many months. DeShawn was in the middle of a personal favor, and it sure didn't sound as if he was enjoying that favor alone. A woman's shrieking moans pierced Adalia's ears, along with the squeak of bouncing bedsprings.

That bastard.

Here she was stressing about telling him she was in love with Trent and he was in the throes of some sordid sex act with God knew who.

Adalia tightened her grip on her handbag and walked into the living room. There were bags of weed and cocaine everywhere. Fury pulsed alongside her beating heart, and she stormed through to the bedroom and crashed inside.

"What the fuck, DeShawn?" She folded her arms and stared at him.

The woman was on top of him, and she shrieked and slid sideways, then covered herself up with his ratty sheets. DeShawn struggled up and his drug-addled confusion turned to horror.

"Daly, it's not what you think, baby, she just a friend." He covered his fast-wilting hard-on and leapt out of bed.

"Hey!" the woman, who had long braids and perky breasts, yelled. "I ain't just a friend."

"Really?" Adalia rubbed her eyes with her thumb and forefinger. "Really. You're going with that lamest excuse in the book?"

"I- I," he started, then paused and pointed at the naked woman. "Get the fuck outta my place, bitch."

"Fuck you, DeShawn," she spat, then dropped the sheet, gathered her heels and what looked to be a mini and tank top and charged out. A door banged shut a moment later, and the apartment fell into relative quiet.

"See, she nothin' to me, Dalie. She nothin'."

Adalia feigned a fluttering heart, pressing her palm to her chest. "Oh, DeShawn, you shouldn't have. I'm so honored you kicked out your cheap lay for me."

"Please, you gotta understand," he said, reaching out to her.

Adalia backed out of the bedroom door. "You really don't." And she meant it too. He didn't have to explain anything to her, because what happened in his personal life was not her problem anymore.

She'd been scared of him and she'd had to face her demons by coming to see him. She'd had to prove that she wasn't afraid of what he thought was his 'power'. It helped that she'd tucked a Taser into her purse to drive the message home if he got frisky.

But DeShawn was on the back foot. "I didn't want her like I want you, girl," he said.

She snorted. "I don't care what you want, DeShawn. I came here as a favor, actually, because I thought you deserved an explanation."

"Huh?" He scratched his forehead and it wrinkled in that trademark DeShawn frown.

"I felt I led you on by going on a date with you, and then seeing Trent afterward, but I think we don't operate under the same rules. It seems you get to do whatever the fuck you want, and still claim me as your woman."

DeShawn was quiet for a moment. "Well, yeah."

"Sorry, sweetheart, but it doesn't work that way. I have no interest in being with you, most specifically because I am in love with Trent Dawson."

"What?!" DeShawn strode forward and she whipped the Taser out. He stopped immediately and stared at it. "What the fuck that for?"

She clicked the switch up then pressed the button, and the non-lethal weapon crackled with electricity. "That's what the fuck it's for."

"Dalie, get real, girl. You ain't gonna shock me."

"I will if you take another step in my direction. I need you to understand this, right now, DeShawn, I'm not your woman and I don't think I ever was." She walked backward into the living room and stared at the drugs. "You've lied to me about this and so many other things. I'm done seeing you around."

"I'm sorry," he muttered, but it was more out of reluctance than genuine remorse. Those sirens grew closer, maybe an ambulance or a cop car. Regardless, someone was dead or injured in the near vicinity.

"I don't care what you are. DeShawn, I'm going to make this clear to you. If you come near me again, I will shock you. And if you come near me after that, I'll buy a damn gun for self-defense." She jabbed the Taser in his direction to punctuate her words with meaning.

"What the fuck?" DeShawn clutched his wrists and rolled his head around.

"You heard me. I never want to see your face again." Adalia turned and walked to the front door, then opened it and strode down the hall, the stairs and into the lot. That drug dealer was there, but his smile vanished at the sight of the Taser in her hand.

She unlocked the car, started it and idled for a second, breathing hard. Then a slow smile spread on her face. She'd done it.

Adalia had gotten her groove back.

Chapter Sixteen

The tables were covered with white cloth and there were ornamental flower arrangements at the center of each, spouting arum lilies in tall glass tubes. There were blue lights inset in the hard wood flooring, but they reminded Adalia of a spaceship rather than setting the tone for a classy wedding.

Still, it was their first wedding. To cater, of course, and she was overwhelmed with excitement. They'd spent hours preparing the tiered cake, garnishing it with realistic icing petals made from pure white fondant.

Everything was in cool blues and white, with a touch of silver for good measure. Adalia wrinkled her nose and turned from the swinging steel door that led into the kitchen. She strode to the freezer and checked the cake through its glass front, then pressed the digital button on the panel and ensured the temperature was exactly right.

Too hot and it would be melted, too cold and the guests would break their teeth on the bakery's creation.

The wedding would begin soon, and Adalia was dressed appropriately in a slimming pale blue dress. She wanted to fit in, not stand out, but Trent was out there amidst the honored guests and it made her heart beat that much faster.

They'd prepared an extra dessert for the guests in case they didn't want the wedding cake, and she stopped beside Jenny and placed a hand on her shoulder.

"Everything going okay?" Adalia squeezed and Jenny shot her a smile brimming with confidence.

"Okay, hah, everything is perfect. The macaroons are flawless, blueberry filling is smooth, we're totally waxed. This is going to impress a lot of people, Adalia." Jenny folded her arms and looked around the gleaming kitchen at the other workers.

"And that means a lot more business," Adalia replied. This was the beginning of a big business endeavor. Maybe she and Trent could start a name brand, as recognizable as Starbucks. Hope swelled in her chest.

"Cheesecakes out in five," Jenny called, checking her silver watch.

Adalia patted her a last time then wandered off through the kitchen and out to take her seat at one of the tables in the reception area. Trent was nearby, chatting to an elderly gentleman in a suit and tie, but her place marker was right beside his. It was, unfortunately, right across from Michelle Van Heerden's as well.

The woman sat there in her top heavy, blonde-haired glory. She raised a hand and twiddled her fingers at Adalia with a dead expression.

"Nice to see you've come up in the world," Michelle said, dripping with sarcasm.

"Nice to see you haven't," Adalia shot back, but Van Heerden didn't rise to the taunt. She simply smiled back and flicked her blonde hair over her shoulder to reveal the silky black number she had on underneath.

Trent strolled over and took a seat beside Adalia, then squeezed her hand gently. He leaned in and brushed her neck with his fingers. "I missed you."

Michelle Van Heerden's smile disappeared instantly.

Jenny appeared in the doorway and rolled the cake out, then positioned it in front of the guests, so they could 'ooh' and 'ah' appropriately.

The bride and groom entered the reception hall and the guests applauded them onto the wooden dance floor for their first dance as a married couple. A band struck a tune, man and wife clasped hands and stared into each other's eyes, and Adalia's insides went squirmy.

She'd never been wedding obsessed, but this kind of thing got to a girl. She swept a tear from under her eyelid and checked that Trent hadn't seen. He hadn't. He stared at a spot over her shoulder, face reddening and jaw clenched tight.

"What's wrong?" Adalia whispered then waggled his arm. "Trent?"

He didn't say a word and she spun in the white ladder back chair. DeShawn stood there, in his sweat-stained tank top and low slung jeans. He was sober as a judge, but angry as she'd ever seen him.

"Hey, bitch," he yelled, and Adalia started. Guests turned, searching for the source of the commotion.

"Get him out of here, before I kill him," Trent grunted. This was huge. This was an opportunity to impress other clients. Adalia scraped her chair back and stood, hurrying forward to face her ex-boyfriend.

"You think you can tell me what you gonna do and I just go wit' it?" DeShawn uttered from spit-froth lips.

"This is not the time. You need to leave, now," Adalia said, surveying the heads of the guests. Most of them watched the dancing couple with vapid smiles or tear-streaked cheeks. Some of the younger women dabbed at the corners of their eyes with silk napkins.

"I ain't goin' nowhere," DeShawn yelled, and the band faltered mid-tune, then continued. Almost every head turned to them this time, including the bride and groom, who frowned and squinted.

This was a disaster.

"Get out of here," she hissed, flapping her arms at him. She didn't have the Taser or anything that could properly discourage him. Maybe he'd figured as much – how had he found her?

"Fuck you!" DeShawn spat. "You can't get away from me that easy."

"Stop it, you can't do this here. Let's go into the kitchen where we can talk, calmly." Adalia patted the air to soothe him. If she could get him out of the limelight, they'd be able to salvage the situation.

"I wanna talk, right here, right now."

"Just keep your voice down, this is a wedding," she whispered back.

DeShawn raised both of his middle fingers. "You're a cheap ho! That's all I gotta say to you." Then he charged past her and up to the mountain of white fondant and cake that had taken over seventy-two hours to perfect.

"No!" Adalia shrieked, sprinting to catch up to him, but he was too far ahead.

The band quieted immediately, and the bride gasped, throwing a hand tipped in perfectly manicured fingernails up to cover her mouth. Trent jerked out his chair… Michelle Van Heerden let out a harsh giggle.

DeShawn grabbed fistfuls of the cake and tore into it, ripping it apart, and Adalia's heart sank through the floor. They'd never recover from this. The bride screamed and actually stumbled backward on her heels. The groom caught her and held her upright.

Trent rushed for DeShawn. If he hit the wannabe dealer, it would be over for their business. The news would travel too fast in the right circles.

"Stop, don't do it," Adalia said, jumping into his path. She grabbed Trent by the upper arms and he halted his charge.

"You're defending him?!" Trent's nostrils were flared, his hair fell across his forehead and tufted with each forced exhalation.

"I'm defending us. If you hit him, it's over, Trent. Come on. Think about this for a moment." She darted left then right, blocking his attempts to get around her.

"I don't want to think about anything. That bastard's been up in our business for too long, now. This is the end. If you don't end this, I'll end him."

Adalia spun and hurried up to the cake, which was already ruined, then grabbed her ex-boyfriend by the forearm. He flicked her off and almost elbowed her in the face, but she managed to dodge the blow.

"Stop this, you've made your point, it's ruined. The entire wedding is ruined. Just stop it, DeShawn," she half-yelled and half-pleaded with him, but he didn't slow his scrunching.

The bride and groom figurines fell from the top and shattered on the silver plate. She'd handed crafted those in their likeness from actual dress rehearsal pictures.

"Snap out of it!" she demanded, making another grab for him.

DeShawn shoved with both hands and the cake splatted onto the dance floor, sending a cascade of cake, fondant, cream and flowers in a stream across the wood. Everything went silent.

"That's what you get," DeShawn yelled, breathing like a winded rhinoceros, "for being a fucking slut." Then he stormed across the hall and slammed out of the building.

The bride fainted. The groom swore. Adalia stared into space, unblinking, and Trent turned his back on her and walked through the kitchen.

Chapter Seventeen

"I didn't mean for that to happen." Adalia stood before Trent with her arms at her side and her head bowed slightly. She was cowed. DeShawn had ruined too much of their business and interfered in her life.

"I don't want to talk about this," he replied, pouring himself a shot of whiskey behind his bar in the mansion. He downed it, then glugged more of the golden liquid into the glass. "I'm tired of talking, seeing and even thinking about goddamn DeShawn."

He didn't even sound that angry, just defeated and that made it so much worse. Adalia joined him at the bar and slid onto a stool. He poured her a drink, a vodka cranberry, and pushed it over. She picked a transparent red-tinted swizzle stick from a holder against the wall and stirred it, then licked the end and plopped it back into the liquid.

"You realize that we won't get business from any of those people," Trent stated, and this time he got a tumbler and put some ice in it, before sloshing whiskey onto the rocks. "We can pretty much write off a lot of profit because of that little stunt."

"I thought you didn't want to talk about it," said Adalia. She sipped her drink, but she wasn't up to it that evening.

"I changed my damn mind. Man, you said he wouldn't be a problem anymore, but that's all that he is. He's tearing everything apart and you're allowing it." Trent pounded his fist on the sleek marble bar top.

"I'm allowing it," she said, tasting the concept on her tongue, though it didn't sit well with the cranberry. "I'm allowing it."

"Yes, you are."

"I'm not allowing anything, Trent. Good God, I went to his apartment the other day and threatened him with a damn Taser so he'd butt out of my life." She hadn't meant to tell him, but she couldn't keep the information in, any longer.

"You did what? Have you lost your damn mind, Adalia?" Trent shoved the glass aside and the ice cubes rattled.

"I did what I had to do. I couldn't let him come between us."

Trent came around the bar and stood in front of her, shaking his head. "You didn't have to take what I said literally. I don't care about DeShawn, I don't care if he crops up twenty million times in the next year, but I do care about your safety."

Adalia drew in a gasp. She'd allowed herself to become so vulnerable with him, but she couldn't help embracing it. There was nothing she wanted more than to be with him every day, all day. He drove her crazy. "I thought you wanted him out of the picture."

"Of course I do," he replied, "but not at the cost of your safety." He touched her cheek then came in for a kiss. She melted for him, and shivers crawled across her skin. She broke away for a moment and he tilted his head to the side, studying her.

"I'm sorry for all of this," she whispered, then squared her shoulders and tried to let go of the guilt.

He cupped her face in his hands and smiled at her. "I want you."

"Now?" Adalia asked, arousal flooding her as soon as he said it.

Trent parted her legs on the stool and hiked up her skirt, then slotted himself in between her thighs. He had a raging hard on already, and she gulped, unable to say a word. He looked down at her and his mouth fell open.

"Adalia, you naughty girl, you're not wearing any panties." Trent's voice was thick with desire.

"I'm your naughty girl," she replied, pressing her breasts against his pecs, and shimmying slightly.

Trent groaned and slipped his hand between her legs, then worked it up her thigh, stroking and gripping her flesh. "You know just what I like." He parted her wet lips and slid a finger inside her, then bent to kiss her neck.

Adalia arched her back slightly and then leaned back to allow him full access. He gripped her around the waist and lowered her so he could get what he wanted, full access to her body. He ripped her dress down and exposed her breasts.

Her brown nipples were fully erect and he moaned again, then took one in his mouth and sucked. Pleasure took her, lifting her high, and she gripped handfuls of his hair, holding on for dear life.

Trent rammed his fingers inside her, grunting with each movement. He nibbled her nipple. "Fuck, I can't even handle this. I need to be inside you."

"Then get inside me, now!" Adalia demanded, and he unzipped his pants and dropped them. He didn't bother stepping out, just parted her lips and plunged inside her, still holding her upper body so she was angled perfectly.

The stool wobbled beneath her and they rocked with the motion. He slowed down so they could enjoy it and she felt everything. The curve of his head stroked her G-spot and she shook from the pleasure, gasping and massaging her own breasts.

"You're so beautiful," he murmured, then pulled out of her and helped her off the stool. "Come with me."

Adalia took his hand and he led her through the house as he had so many months ago, up the stairs and into his bedroom, the absence of incomprehensible maids apparent, thank god. He laid her down on the sheets then stood over her, staring.

"What?"

"I'm just admiring you," he replied, stroking his shaft slowly, running his hand over it then just a finger, then with purpose, watching her reaction. She chewed her lip then sucked it and he went faster.

Adalia couldn't stand it anymore, she crawled onto her knees in front of him, and his eyes widened. She took him in her mouth and sucked, moaning as she did. Trent gripped her head and growled. He was huge, and her jaw hurt after a few seconds.

"That's amazing," he stammered, legs weakening. His knees buckled but he straightened again and braced himself with one hand on the wall. "Fuck, that's too good."

Adalia stopped for a second, but replaced her mouth with her hand and stroked him. "Don't you dare come," she replied, then ensconced him between her lips once more.

"I'm close," he grunted, thrusting into her, and she turned over and presented herself instead.

"Fill me up. I want all of you inside me." She parted her ass cheeks so he could see how wet she was. Trent didn't need a second invitation. He pounded into her, losing any semblance of control.

His movement was bestial and he gripped her hip so hard it hurt, but she loved it. The sensation of his body smacking into hers, while she shrieked for more. He throbbed inside her, growing larger as he approached his climax.

Adalia reached between her legs and fingered her clit in circles. She collapsed with her ass in the air and he came hard. She shattered at the same moment, rocking with the waves of pleasure.

Their bodies meshed into one. She was with him and it felt right, better than the last time, than the first time. Trent slid out of her an eternity later, and lay down on the bed beside her. She couldn't move.

"I love you, Adalia," he murmured, eyes falling closed slowly. How could she have doubted him? The fear and pain, the jealousy was a distant memory. "No matter what, I love you," he said.

"I love you, too," she managed, finally sinking down onto her stomach. She admired his jawline, the growth of stubble on his chin, the rise and fall of his chest. He was her perfection, everything a man should be.

"Be mine forever," he said, and she giggled at the sweet sentiment. "I'm serious."

"You're all doped up on sex," she replied.

Then he curled her into his arms, tucked her onto his heart and fell asleep with his lips pressed to her forehead. She'd never been as happy.

Adalia Montclair was complete.

Chapter Eighteen

"Adalia," Trent whispered into her ear, and a smile lifted the corners of her mouth.

"I love waking up to you," she murmured, then turned to put her arm across his brawny chest. But it hit linen instead, and she cracked an eyelid. Trent wasn't in the bed, but stood beside it in a loose white T-shirt and a pair of worn in jeans.

He had one hand behind his back and the other in his pocket, with his hip cocked to the side like a male model.

"What are you doing?" She drew the word out with a groan. "Come back to bed right this minute."

"Sorry, my love, I can't do that. You need to get out of bed. We have some serious issues to discuss." His grin faltered, then straightened, and he took his hand out of his pocket and rubbed his palm down the left side of his leg.

Adalia sat up, anxiety feathering through her chest. "What issues? Should I be worried? Is it DeShawn, did he –?"

Trent's chuckle burst out of his mouth, but cut off short. "Relax, Adalia, but please do get out of bed, so we can talk about this."

She swallowed hard, then slid her legs over the edge of the bed, and swung herself upright. If she had to get out of bed for this, it couldn't be good.

"Trent, I –"

He dropped to his knee before she could get another word out, and the world ceased to exist.

"What are you doing?" Adalia breathed, grasping at her naked chest. Good God, she didn't have any clothes on.

"Quiet, I love you." Trent's tone brooked no complaints. "I've been thinking about this for a really long time, planning it for almost as long. I need you to know how I feel inside, because sometimes I don't think it comes across right."

Adalia couldn't do anything but stare into his eyes and get lost in this insane, breathless moment. There were birds chirping somewhere, probably bees humming too. Nothing mattered.

"Adalia, you're the most amazing woman I've ever met. You're sassy, but vulnerable at the same time, and you make me feel like a man. I can only hope that I make you feel like a woman too. I plan on doing it for the rest of my life." He broke off and brought a maroon velvet box out from behind his back.

Trent popped the lid and exposed a ring. Adalia gasped. The diamond was nestled between two curling bands of platinum metal frosted with tiny sparkling gems.

"Adalia Montclair, will you marry me?"

'Yes' was the only answer to that question. Maybe even 'hell yes'.

"Trent –"

Bang!

"What the fuck do you think you're doing, *Mr. Dawson*?" Michelle Van Heerden crashed into the room with her hair drawn up in a high ponytail, strands sticking out at odd angles, creating a twisted halo that didn't suit her personality.

"Michelle?" Trent turned, in utter confusion.

Van Heerden's eyes traveled to Adalia's naked chest, and the corners of her lips curled upward in disdain. Adalia grasped the sheet and pulled it around herself.

"Did you forget me, darling?" Michelle asked, tone dripping sarcasm. "I would've thought that yesterday afternoon was etched into your damn memory."

"Yesterday afternoon?" Adalia asked, and her stomach did a miniature trampoline belly flop.

"That's right, yesterday afternoon," Michelle replied.

Trent shook his head, but snapped the lid of the box shut and then rose from his knees. "You're interrupting an important event, Ms. Van Heerden, and that interruption will cost you your job if you don't leave this instant."

But Michelle didn't leave. If anything, her grin grew wider. She reached into her handbag and brought out her cell, then swiped her thumb across the screen. She charged forward and held it out at arm's length, facing Adalia.

An image presented itself. Michelle in nothing but a thong and bra, straddling Trent. It destroyed Adalia's perceptions of the man she loved.

"This happened yesterday." Van Heerden blinked at her, and Trent dove for the phone, but his assistant snatched it back to her chest.

"That's not possible," Adalia whispered, but the truth had already sunk in. Trent had left after the wedding… maybe he'd been with Michelle before they'd met up at his mansion. That had to be the answer.

He'd cheated on her and realized she'd find out. That was why he'd proposed. He wanted to lock her down before she found out. She stood and searched the room for her underwear and clothes. They were strewn across the carpet. Trent moved to block her path toward them.

"This is bullshit." Trent ripped the phone from Michelle and tossed it at the wall, shattering it into pieces. The battery flew one way and the screen the other. "Michelle, you're fired."

"I don't care, as long as we can be together, Trent." Van Heerden fluttered a smile, and Adalia's nausea rose in a tide. She clapped her hand to her mouth and swallowed the extra saliva reflexively.

This was a waking nightmare.

"Get the fuck out of my house, right now." Trent trembled with rage, bare biceps lined with veins.

Michelle folded her arms. "I'm not going anywhere."

"How could you do it?" Adalia asked, staring at the billionaire. There was sunlight now, streaming in and lighting the bed they'd slept in, where they'd spent hours of the night worshipping each other's bodies.

"I didn't touch that woman," he growled.

"The photos say otherwise." Adalia didn't let the tears come yet. She'd wait until she was out of the mansion, in her loaned car. Loaned from the guy who'd fucked his assistant the day before he proposed to her.

"Yeah, yesterday he was so angry, I took him out for a couple drinks, and one thing led to another. It's not like you ever really deserved him." Michelle spread her arms in a forgiving gesture, as if this was Adalia's fault she'd gotten in the way of Michelle and Trent's relationship.

Trent charged at Michelle, who shrieked and hopped out of the way. She raced around to the other side of the bed, and cowered, though Adalia didn't buy the fear for a second. This drama was exactly what Michelle wanted.

She was a liar, but the photos couldn't lie. They had to be real.

"I'm leaving," Adalia said out loud to the room more than to either of them. Trent stopped midstride – marching to Michelle – and turned back. That velvet box poked out from the gap in his fist, between his thumb and forefinger.

"You can't leave. I love you."

"Don't lie anymore, Trent. It's over. I don't know what your motivation was for this whole charade, but if you loved me, you wouldn't have had sex with her. It's as simple as that." Adalia gritted her teeth and strolled to the door, inserting casual grace into her stride that she didn't feel.

She swept her clothes up along the way. She'd change in the bathroom before her hasty escape.

Trent rushed back to her side and took her hand, but she tore it away from him, channeling her rage into that single motion. He actually started and stepped back. "This is insane. I didn't sleep with Michelle. You can't take her word over mine, pictures or not."

"This was a mistake. I keep making the same mistakes over and over again. Just when I think I've got it right…" She laughed at herself, mirthless of course then continued. "It doesn't matter. It's over, Trent. I'm going to move out of your apartment, and I want out of the bakery."

"Please don't go," Trent said, trying for her again. Her heart broke into irreparable fragments as she pulled away from him.

"Goodbye," she replied. Then she walked out of the room, closed the door and changed on the spot, trying but failing to block out Michelle's hysterical laughter and the low grumble of Trent's vicious diatribe.

He didn't bother coming after her, but that was because he'd never cared all that much.

Adalia Montclair wasn't complete anymore, she never had been, and she was utterly broken.

There wasn't enough sunlight to illuminate her path, not with all those tears blurring her vision.

Chapter Nineteen

Adalia lifted her fist to the door then dropped it to her side again. She didn't want to knock. The wrinkled disdain on the other side of that door terrified her more than a future without baking.

Why was that?

Sylvester Montclair's disappointment was a cross she didn't want to bear, but Adalia would be damned if she went back to Trent's apartment for more time than it took to pack her bags and get the hell out of there.

She crunched the handle of the bag in palm and slammed it into her thigh.

"Grow a pair, Adalia," she whispered, then rapped her knuckles against the white wood three times. Her father's footsteps rang out from the other side of the door.

The bolt scraped back and he opened up. His eyebrows danced in surprise.

"What are you doing here, girl?" Sylvester asked, gripping the jamb with clawed fingers. He hadn't cut his nails in a while, but they were immaculately clean. The blanket was nowhere to be seen, and he didn't splutter or cough. He simply stood there, glaring at her.

Fatherly warmth was gone.

"Dad, I need…" she said, then coughed into her fist and slapped the bag into her thigh again.

"You need what, exactly?"

"I need your help." *Man, that hurt like hell.* A direct dig to her pride.

"Well, that's unfortunate, isn't it?" Sylvester's expression hardened so much she could hardly find her father behind the anger. What had she done to deserve this kind of reaction? Hadn't she been a good daughter to him?

"Please, Dad, I have nowhere else to go."

"That's all it's been about," Sylvester murmured as if he'd spoken more to himself than anyone else.

"What?"

"You," her father replied through clenched teeth.

"I have no idea what you mean, Dad."

"You're selfish, you only care about what's best for you and not how you affect others. This is the *Adalia Show* in your eyes," Sylvester barked.

Cool prickles rose on her scalp. "That's not true," she replied. "I tried to help you and pay some of your bills but you wouldn't let me."

"You think that's what this is about? You don't hear yourself talking or something? Every second word is

'I'." Her father shook his head and the anger faded away. He brought out the next best weapon in his arsenal: disappointment.

"This isn't fair. I did my best to make you comfortable while I was here."

"You didn't know I was in financial trouble until your issues cleared up then it was time to check in on Dad and figure out how to 'help' him. I don't need help from you, girl, hence you're the one begging for my help." Sylvester hadn't been cruel growing up, not even when she'd worn her mother's pearls and broken them by accident.

Those pearls had sat in the silk-lined jewelry box on the dressing table in her father's room for years. Adalia had thought it a waste of a perfectly good piece of costume jewelry.

Silly girl.

"I wasn't trying to ignore your issues, Dad. I really do want to help you. I was just so caught up in everything."

"You were caught up in *Adalia Land* doing what you do best. Ignoring everyone who truly cares about you. You moved into some billionaire's apartment and you don't bother calling to check in on me." Sylvester nodded at the truth.

"You told me not to contact you."

"No, I told you not to come back here, but you can't seem to follow simple instructions." Her father let go of the doorjamb and shuffled out a few feet, into the light of midafternoon. He seemed older than the last time, the furrows in his brow were deeper and the wisdom in his eyes was sour.

No, it wasn't wisdom at all, rather cynicism. He'd past the point of hope for the world, maybe he'd seen too much on that damn TV. Maybe she was the reason he'd lost faith. There were too many memories of her childhood, but they were blurred by her need to win where her brothers had lost.

She'd been so focused on doing the right thing that she'd left relationships in her wake. There wasn't an easy way to repair them. Mike might put her up if she asked real nice. Adalia used her finger to swipe for tears beneath either eye, but her skin was dry.

"I'll leave," she said despondently. She spun on her heel, bag flapping against her thigh, carrying the weight of her clothes and shoes, the only possessions she had to her name. The car was gone too.

"Don't be stupid." Her father's words made her fragmented heart ache worse. "You can stay here if you need to, just don't talk to me. I've got no interest in discussing your issues until you realize you're the sole cause of them."

He went inside and left her there, but didn't close the door. Tears welled up from her eyes. She was 'welcome' inside until further notice apparently. Icy air gushed from the open doorway, brushing her cheeks and drying out her lips.

There was her father's threshold, waiting to accept her but not truly embrace her. He'd loved her at the beginning, hadn't he?

Adalia wasn't sure who she meant: Trent or Sylvester.

She braced herself for the weeks of hard living. She'd have to find another job, maybe go back to that damn market. A car sped past, bass pumping loud enough to make the windows buzz in their frames.

Stray dogs barked in the distance, nosing through spilled trash on the corner. Children giggled and tripped over a skipping rope. The usual sights she'd seen year after year, but it didn't comfort her.

Adalia walked into the arctic depths of her father's home. She went through to the bedroom, which lay open and empty but for the comforter on the bed and a naked desk in the corner.

She shut the bedroom door and rifled through her handbag for her cell. She needed that old school comfort, that feeling of belonging and she hated herself for it.

Adalia went through her contacts absentmindedly, then exited and dialed his number without real thought for the consequences.

"What the fuck you want, bitch?" DeShawn answered, with his usual elegance.

"I need to talk to you. Things have gotten out of hand and I thought we could talk it out." Adalia loathed the words that dribbled from her mouth, useless as drool. She was useless. She felt low to call him when she'd backed out of a relationship with him.

She reached into the bag and touched the Taser, flicking the button back and forth, but it didn't remind her of anger or hatred, only pity. She pitied herself.

"I got nothing to say to you."

"DeShawn, wait, please don't hang up on me. I've got no one else to talk to right now," Adalia pleaded.

"What 'bout your pretty boy?"

"We broke up. It's over. He cheated on me and I didn't even see it coming." Adalia gripped her forehead with her palm to still the trembling. That didn't help.

"He cheat on you?" DeShawn asked, and she could hear the smile in his voice.

"That's what I said," she replied, and he blew out brusque laughter in her ear. That was the soundtrack to her misery.

"You got what you deserve, girl," DeShawn said. Adalia squished the phone, mashing it into her cheek. "You a fat bitch who can't do nothin' right."

She couldn't reply to that, but he didn't leave her the option. The line went dead a second later. Adalia dropped the phone to the bedspread and lay back, stretching her arms above her head then bringing them to rest below her breasts, clasping them in the front as if she were on her way to the grave.

There was no deeper hell than to turn to an ex-boyfriend for help and be rejected. This was her lowest level. She'd hit rock bottom and she didn't want to sink through to the center of the earth.

Chapter Twenty

Adalia and Mike sat in his navy blue BMW 335i Coupe and stared at the hot dog mini-cart across the road. She'd already spilled ketchup on her blouse, but licking the napkin had only made the paper soggy and left little rolls of tissue all down her front.

"I'm glad we could have this chat," Mike said, chomping down on the end of his dog. He didn't spill a single drop of mustard, his leather seats were flawless, and he wasn't jumpy about her messier eating habits.

"You spoke to Dad, didn't you?" Adalia asked around a mouthful of meat and bun. She'd had two already and a third was perched precariously on his dash. A line trailed out from the mini-cart, mothers clutching their children, fathers yawing, businessmen compulsively checking their watches.

Mike didn't have to answer the question. The lack of reply was answer enough.

"I had to get out of there before he consumed me." Adalia placed her half-eaten hotdog beside the third one and sighed.

"Who? Trent Dawson or Dad?"

She'd asked that question herself. "Trent, of course," she said to her brother.

"So what do you need me for, sis? If you've already extricated yourself, I won't be of much service to you."

"I need an ear, a rock, someone who gets it and can offer me proper advice." Adalia drummed her heels. Her father was right; she was selfish. "But how are you, Mike? Are things going well at the firm?"

Mike squeezed his eyes shut for a moment. "I'm tired. I love what I do, but I'm tired of work. I need a vacation soon."

After years of studying and pouring everything he had into his job, Adalia couldn't think of anyone who deserved a break more than Mike Montclair.

"I see," she replied, then shoved more of the hotdog into her mouth. It tasted like ash now that the subject of their dad came up.

"Do you need legal advice?" He turned, squeaking on the leather to face her. He was such an honest man and a good brother. He really wanted to help her for no personal gain. What did that say about her?

"Kind of. Trent and I broke up, and I moved out of the apartment he leased to me, but getting out of the bakery…" Adalia trailed off and crumpled up the wrapper, but didn't have anywhere to toss it, so she put into her bag beside the first.

"Ah, you signed a contract. Well, if he allows you to leave, you can render that contract null and void."

Mike crumpled up his paper, buzzed down his window and tossed it into the nearby trash can.

"Yeah, except he won't let me out of the damn contract. He wants me to work with him, regardless of everything that's transpired." Adalia grappled a bite of the third hot dog into her jaws and munched away.

Mike tapped his fingers on the steering wheel. "He won't let you out. That's weird."

"Yeah, he's a persistent man. He's set on torturing me or something," she said.

Mike fell silent for a while, watching the passerby on the street, smiling softly at a young mother pushing her baby in its pink-frilled stroller. He was gentle at the best of times, but he had a darker side, an anger that Adalia had seen once.

She'd been bullied a lot as a kid. Once they'd cornered her against the swings and the older girls had pulled her pigtails until some of her hair actually tore away from her scalp. They'd called her fat and made snorting noises.

That was when Mike had appeared. He'd swept them aside as if they were nothing more than dust. He hadn't screamed but she'd never forget the expression he'd worn that day. Liquefied rage spilling from his muscles.

"Why did you break up? Who broke up with whom?" Mike finally spoke, turning analytical eyes on her.

"He cheated. I don't want to talk about it." Adalia slammed the hotdog down, crushing it on the dash, and Mike finally grimaced. He removed it and threw it into the trash can to join his empty wrapper.

"Tell me what happened," he said, patiently.

"Hey, I was gonna eat that," she replied, frowning at her brother. He always thought he knew better, but that was because he did.

"Cut the crap and start talking, Adalia." Mike placed his hand on the back of her headrest.

"I told you I don't want to talk about this, so why are you forcing the damn issue?"

"Because that's my privilege as the older sibling," he said, with a wry smile. "And because I genuinely care about you. I can't assess this situation properly without full knowledge of what actually occurred."

Adalia swept it around in her mind. Mike was a big help. What harm was there in discussing her issues with him when she couldn't deal with them by herself?

"All right fine," she said with an almighty sigh. "I fell for him even though I shouldn't have. He seemed like a good guy, but he turned out to be a sleazebag like most men his age. Worse even because he made me believe he felt for me, too. He even proposed."

"He what now?!" Mike never yelled except when he was genuinely surprised.

"Yeah, he got down on one knee with a ring and everything. Princess cut, goddamn it." That ring was stunning. Her heart ached all over again.

"That doesn't sound like the typical cheating spouse," Mike observed. "Those kinds of guys, and trust me I've dealt with plenty of them in my profession, don't usually fork out hard-earned cash to marry a woman. They're more likely to take you on a vacation to the Bahamas or something."

"Huh?"

"I don't know… that's just what they do," Mike replied, shrugging off the facts.

"What has this got to do with anything?" Adalia glared at the trash can that had eaten her last hot dog. She had a serious case of the 'comfort eats' as her father had liked to call them.

"It's just not typical cheating behavior. Anyway, how do you know he cheated on you?"

"I saw it for myself."

Mike's mouth curled downward in distaste. "You walked in on him with another woman?"

"No, no, the other woman turned up and showed me a pic she snapped on her phone. Her, naked and on top of him. God it was awful," Adalia whispered, clasping her cheeks with either hand.

"Wait a sec, she showed you a pic?" Mike shook his head. "Adalia, have you ever heard of Photoshop before?"

"How are you on his side right now?" Adalia growled at her brother and dropped her hands into her lap again. She whacked down the sun visor to block out the light.

"Because you're being ridiculous. You have absolutely no proof that he did anything with that woman other than some picture that could've been a few years old. Tell me you checked the details on it," he replied.

Adalia chewed the inside of her cheek. "I might not have."

"Oh, Adalia," he said in the way he did when she'd done something particularly dumb but didn't want to say it out loud.

"There was still proof he'd been with her though." Adalia tried to defend it, but he continued shaking his head.

"Seriously, that's a rookie mistake. Why would you believe her word over his? She has more incentive to break you guys up than he does." Mike clicked the button on his arm rest and his window slid closed. "I don't think you should get out of the contract at the bakery."

"Why not?" Adalia fastened her seatbelt. Mike started the car then drove down the road, ever so slowly.

"Because you owe him an apology." Mike steered toward the bakery. Adalia's heart leapt into her throat, beating at a furious pace.

"I loved him and he…" Had he truly betrayed her? She had to find out for sure, or maybe she didn't. Things were so confused.

"Clear your mind, sister, because you've got a lot of explaining to do. God knows, if I was Trent, I'm not sure I'd allow you back into my life. But that's just me." Mike parked and left the car to idle.

"Wish me luck." Adalia opened the car door and swung her feet out.

Mike gave her a friendly pat on the shoulder. "Sure. You're going to need it."

Chapter Twenty-One

Jenny's mouth dropped open the second Adalia strolled through the kitchen door.

"Don't look so surprised," she muttered to her old friend and colleague.

"Sorry, it's not that I'm surprised. I hope this means you'll be coming back to work, because things haven't been as fluid without you here." Jenny squeezed her shoulder.

"Where is he?" Adalia asked, reaching up to grip her friend's hand. She had to do this before she got the chance to chicken out. Too much had passed between them now, and there wasn't any going back.

Jenny hesitated then nodded to herself. "He's through there, but I gotta warn you, kid. He's been in a foul mood every time he's come in here... although he hasn't come by as much since you left."

"Yeah, sorry for that. I'll deal with it, don't worry," Adalia replied then waved Jenny off with a weak smile.

The office door was a few feet away, but it took an eternity to get there. Each step was three breaths long. Three very quick breaths in succession, then she'd lift her other foot and do the same.

She felt like Armstrong on the moon, taking the first small steps for mankind. Except these were for forgiveness, not that she'd necessarily get it.

Adalia stopped in front of the door and knocked once, softly.

"What do you want?" Trent yelled inside. "I'm busy in here."

She let herself in and pressed the door shut behind her, leaning her back against it to study his reaction. He didn't seem happy.

"I came to talk about what happened."

"For once, I don't feel like talking to you, Adalia. I don't want to see you at all." Trent shuffled a pile of papers together, patted them on their end and stored them in a tray on the edge of the desk.

Adalia cleared her throat. "I know I've been a jerk. I realize that."

"That's a first," he replied, but his tone had softened slightly. He ruffled that blond hair and popped his collar, then smoothed it down again. There was no tie today either, and he was decidedly frazzled. His nails weren't as neat, not cut but bitten maybe.

Trent had taken strain.

"You look haggard," she said.

"Thanks," he replied, "you don't look like a million bucks either, but you don't see me rubbing it in."

"You just did." Adalia finally parted from the door and went to take a seat in the chair across from his. "I want to know the truth about Michelle Van Heerden. But most of all I want to say sorry for jumping to conclusions so fast. I guess I expect the worst because then I'll be less disappointed when it actually happens."

"Have a little faith in me, Adalia. I'm not your fucking enemy," Trent snapped, then reeled in the anger.

"It's difficult for me, but I'll be better, I swear it." Adalia pressed her lips together and let them unglue themselves into a pout. She was so unsure of this and everything else. She needed to be sure of him. She needed that sense of security.

"To answer your question," he said, then traced a circle on the wood of the desk. Adalia sensed from the creases on his forehead that he was thinking about what he'd say next. "Michelle is nothing but an assistant. I've been aware of her desire to get me into bed for a while, however."

Anger flared again and Adalia slapped her thighs. "So why keep her on?"

"A favor to her father and because I have no physical attraction to her whatsoever," Trent replied, matter-of-factly.

"But what about the picture of you two together, or the time I walked in on you with her at your place?" Adalia asked.

"That's the same day, I assume. She took that picture when I was at my most vulnerable. I was drunk as hell, Adalia. I was upset because of you and she took her chance to make her move. I didn't do anything with her."

Adalia's thoughts flashed back and forth, then settled on the night she'd walked in on them together. She squeezed her eyes shut and envisioned the picture. The underwear, that cursed thong, was the same in both cases.

"I'm sorry I didn't give you a chance to explain," she said.

"It's all right. I understand why you'd think the worst. She's an abrasive woman at the best of times."

Their conversation faded into nothingness, the separation of space was consumed by silence. Adalia needed to be closer.

Trent scooched forward in his chair and leaned over the desk. "I don't want you to leave the bakery."

"I have to. I can't be here with you when there's history between us. It's not professional," Adalia said.

Trent pushed himself out of the chair and came around to her side of the desk, then got down on both knees in front of her. He rested his palms on her knees.

"What if there wasn't a history between us? What if there was a future?"

"What?" she asked, not daring to hope that he would still want her.

"Here's the deal. I love you. I want to marry you. I want to be with you for the rest of our natural lives and I want to run this bakery together." Trent retrieved that box from his pocket and took the ring out of it, then tossed the velvet case aside. There wasn't a question this time. He grasped her left hand and slid the engagement ring onto her finger.

"I, oh God, Trent. I don't know what to say." Adalia gasped for air, her pulse pounding in her throat.

"Yes would be good."

"Yes, I'll marry you. I'll be your wife." That was the most amazing sentence she'd ever uttered. He enclosed her cheeks in his massive hands and brought her lips to his for a gentle kiss. He sucked her bottom lip then kissed her nose and both her eyes.

"I love you. I want this to be our forever."

They stood together and he towered over her, wrapping her in his strong arms and sheltering her from the fear of failure in their love life at last.

"This means you'll continue at the bakery, too," Trent stated, then tucked her hair behind her ear and kissed her lobe.

"No, I'm not sure about that."

"Aren't we past the whole charity thing yet? This is me. You're allowed to be vulnerable with me." Trent smooshed his lips onto her forehead this time.

"This isn't about charity or handouts." She tugged back and looked up at him, drinking in the edge of his jaw and the sharp eyebrows. "I've felt like a failure the past few months. I've been low on self-esteem and it's thrown my judgement off big time."

"But you're not a failure," he said. The frown returned.

"I know that. I'm not a failure," she said out loud, and it felt damn good to voice it. "I'm not a failure, but I do need to establish my independence professionally and financially. You understand that, right?"

Trent considered it for a few minutes. "Yeah, I understand, but working here could help you set yourself up for the future."

"Explain."

"Well, work here and make enough to set yourself up. We'll go from there." Trent smiled, and she appreciated the offer. That would mean setting up in direct competition.

"I don't know." Adalia snaked her arms around his neck and tugged him down for another kiss. He lingered for a while, and she grew warm inside, hot and ready for him. He slipped his hand inside her shirt and tweaked her nipple.

"I do know. You're the one for me, and I want to make you happy. We'll do what it takes. All right?"

Adalia beamed with joy. "All right."

Chapter Twenty-Two

The arch was situated in open air near the ocean, where the breeze tufted the lilies that wound through the framework. There were dark wood chairs, with cream upholstery, laid out in neat rows. The guests chatted amongst themselves, some bursting with laughter, others subdued.

Michelle Van Heerden was nowhere to be seen. Neither was DeShawn.

Adalia let out a long, low sigh and stood in the doorway of the beach house, breathing in the sweet fragrance of baking chocolate buns. Trent's favorite. This was their day, and no one could take that away from them.

Sylvester Montclair was at home, though she'd invited him to the wedding. He'd emailed her back – though it must've taken work given his aversion to technology – that regrettably he was unable to attend due to an unforeseen circumstance, namely that he was ill.

That was a load of crap. He didn't want to be around her and that was that.

"Are you ready for this?" Mike stood beside her in his tux, dashing as only her brother could be.

"I'm beyond ready, Mike. I think I've been waiting for this my entire life." She checked to be sure her hair was fine in the mirror above the walnut table in the hall. It was done up on top of her head, piled and cascading fashionably, with a single Casablanca lily tucked into the curls.

"You look breathtaking," Jenny said, then handed her the bouquet and gave her a swift peck on the cheek. "Oh shit, I've left a lipstick smudge. God forbid Trent thinks you've turned lesbian in the interim."

Adalia laughed, and Jenny flourished a handkerchief and wiped the accusing shade of ruby red lipstick off her cheek.

"I've never seen a man more excited in my life. God, he's practically on vibrate out there." Jenny gestured toward the arch, and Adalia honed in on the man of her dreams. He was outfitted in a smart, tailored black suit and tie. He held onto his cuffs with his fingertips and jerked them every few seconds.

The pastor stood right behind him, going over his sermon or the words, or whatever it was he had to do in a small book with a leather cover. His lips moved as he read. Trent's best man, a business associate she didn't recognize, stood impassively by his side, checking the rose attached to his lapel intermittently.

Trent didn't see her from where he stood, but the view she had was priceless. She took several mental images to be stored away until the day she died, so she could pull them out and dissect them at her leisure.

The wedding band struck up the march and Mike held out his arm to her. She took it with one last breath. She wouldn't be Adalia Montclair for much longer. She relished the thought of becoming Mrs. Trent Dawson.

"You look beautiful, sister. I'm proud to walk you down the aisle today. You've become the woman you always wanted to be. Don't ever doubt that," Mike whispered, as they strolled out of the beach house and onto the cream carpet that led all the way up to Trent on the raised dais.

The guests turned to watch her ascent to Trent, smiles lighting their face. Some of the women dabbed at their eyes. There was her great aunt, over in the corner with an obscene hat perched atop and even more obscene perm. She was a good person, she'd tried to give Adalia money as a wedding gift, and far too much of that.

The flower girl walked ahead, flouncing along with a hop in between steps, tossing lilies left and right a little too enthusiastically. Jenny was just behind her in the open-backed pale pink bridesmaid dress Adalia had selected a week ago.

There hadn't been much time to plan, though she'd done her best. There were lanterns positioned beside the chairs, as there would be in the gazebo positioned closer to the ocean.

Tears welled up, but she didn't try to hold them back this time. Adalia didn't sob, but the liquid rolled down her cheeks, ever so slowly, then dripped onto her décolletage.

She was in a white dress, with transparent lace sleeves and a V-cut that met a white satin bodice. She gripped the flowers in both hands and strolled toward him, wishing she'd get there faster.

Trent's look wasn't lust or desire, but pure love. He shone from his need to be closer to her, illuminating the already sunny day. The waft of wind brought her that lily scent and she inhaled, appreciating it and the taste of sea salt on her lips, where it'd stuck to the pale pink lip gloss.

Finally, after what had to be hours, she halted in front of her groom.

Mike kissed her on the cheek and squeezed her arm once. "Always be strong, don't ever sell out. Believe in who you are, Adalia. It will get you further than hard work."

She blinked at him in consternation. What a strange thing to say when giving her away. She didn't ask what he meant; she accepted it for what it was: Mike's own brand of loving advice. Hard talk mixed with warmth.

Mike tilted toward Trent and she caught his words. "Look after her or you'll have more than the weight of the law to deal with. You get me?"

Trent shook Mike's hand, expression drawn with sincerity. "I'll cherish her until the day I die, and even then."

Mike nodded a last time and transferred Adalia's hand to Trent's. Together, they walked up the stairs of the dais and halted in front of the pastor. They turned to face each other, both grinning from ear to ear.

"You're perfect," he said, lifting her hand to his lips. He grazed her knuckles with a kiss.

"So are you," she countered with a broad smile. She was sorely tempted to kiss him before they'd gotten close to the vows. Waves crashed onto the sands in the distance, brushing the shore in a soft hiss which soothed her.

"Are we ready to begin?" the pastor asked, soft enough that the congregation of guests couldn't hear.

"Absolutely," they replied in unison then smiled at each other again. He was so handsome she might actually cry all over again. Thank God she'd chosen the waterproof mascara. Jenny's suggestion… that girl knew her too well.

"Very well, let us begin," the pastor began, and the audience members straightened and shifted in their seats.

"Not so fucking fast," a voice rang out in the sea breeze and hush. Everyone froze then searched for the source as one. Adalia gritted her teeth. She knew that voice and so did Trent, judging from the way he stiffened.

"I don't believe it," Trent grunted, and fear twanged at the chords of her heart. He couldn't blame her for this. He looked at her, then grabbed her by the arms and drew her into a protective hug. "Don't worry. It's going to be all right."

"Bullshit, it ain't gonna be nothin' but fucked up," DeShawn yelled, charging across the distance and up to the base of the dais.

"Get out of here. You've ruined enough weddings for one year," Adalia said, using a commanding tone she'd perfected in the kitchen and in her relationship with Trent, not that it worked in the latter.

"Not before this asshole knows what you did," DeShawn retorted. His do-rag was back on and those low-hanging jeans and sweat-stained tank top didn't match anything in the area.

"I didn't do anything," Adalia snapped. "Now get out of here."

"Yo, straight up, man to man, I fucked this bitch last night," DeShawn said to Trent, and Adalia's soul shriveled into a ball. She hadn't been anywhere near DeShawn. Her last contact with him was when she'd phoned him in a moment of weakness.

"What?!" Adalia shrieked, and tried to tug away from Trent. She'd kill the bastard for doing this. This was supposed to be her special day!

"Yeah that's right, she moaned like a bitch, too," DeShawn sniffed and wiped his nose with his thumb.

"I can't believe you're doing this," Adalia said.

Trent looked down at her and she met his gaze. "Adalia, is this true?"

-To be continued in Book 3-

If you enjoyed this title, I would appreciate your leaving a review of the book. Good reviews encourage an author to write as well as help books to sell. Good reviews can be just a few short sentences describing what you liked about the book without having a spoiler. If you could spend 30 seconds writing a review, I would appreciate it: you can review this title right now at your favorite retailer.

Here is a preview of the **next book** you may also enjoy:

Love Endured: Tenacious Billionaire BWWM Romance Series, Book 3

ADALIA SAT beside the infinity pool at the Grace Hotel and looked out over the deep blue ocean. Trent was inside, a quick business call to sort out his affairs before their honeymoon got into full swing.

She sighed and a smile parted her lips at the taste of salty sea air. Santorini, Greece had been her choice. The quaint white structures and sloping stairs, the city tucked against the mountain, built from the rock itself, was her idea of a fairytale.

They'd arrived a few hours ago and she itched to go out and explore, but there were matters to attend to before they could go anywhere. It irritated her that Trent took the business calls for the bakery, while she didn't have a true business of her own.

One day, she'd be the one in the expensive hotel room, making the calls, buying and selling and checking in on progress. At least, that was her dream.

"You're quiet, my love," Trent said, strolling from the cool interior and taking a seat beside her. He'd opted for an open neck cotton shirt and white pair of slacks. His tan biceps bulged to free themselves from the sleeves restraining them.

Adalia swallowed, overcome by desire again. Every day with Trent was different, an adventure, but one thing would never change – her need for him.

"How was your call?" Adalia asked, squeezing his hand in hers.

"Oh fine, fine. Just some news on the space frontier. We're going live with the IPO in a couple months, so things are going crazy."

"IPO," she repeated, wriggling her eyebrows. "You're opening the company to trade?"

"It's the next big step. We should've done it years ago. Take a look at SkyLyft. They're trading and apart from the debacle with the crash, they're doing pretty damn well." Trent scratched his chin with the tip of his index finger. "But do you really want to talk business, gorgeous?"

"I want to do many things. Including you," she quipped.

He chuckled and picked up a bottle of champagne from the poolside table. He poured for both of them, then handed her one.

"I think we're overdue for a toast after all the shit we've been through," Trent said, then clinked the rim of his glass against hers.

"I couldn't agree more." She raised the flute to her lips. Nausea bubbled in her stomach and she pulled it away again.

"What's wrong?"

"Nothing… I just feel a little strange. I'm fine, really, don't worry." It was probably the plane food.

They'd served some kind of exotic Indian dish and it hadn't gone down well.

Trent slid his arm around her shoulders and pulled her close. He leaned his head against hers and they looked out over the ocean together. "I couldn't have chosen a better destination myself."

"Oh please, you would've had us hiking in Machu Picchu," she said, then pressed a hand to her stomach. Man, the last thing she needed was to start their honeymoon going down on the toilet. That would almost be as bad as DeShawn's attempt to discredit her at the wedding.

Trent's eyes glistened in the morning light. He tipped his head back and soaked up the sun.

Bile crept up Adalia's throat and she stood abruptly.

"What's wrong?" Trent rose immediately and stroked his fingers down her spine.

"I don't know. I just don't feel well." She managed to stand before the nausea completely overwhelmed her. She slapped her palm across her mouth, turned and sprinted for their room. She crashed through into the pristine white suite and grimaced at the off chance she'd let loose before she hit the bathroom.

Adalia skidded around the corner and slid into the bathroom. She didn't have time to close the door. She crouched over the toilet and let breakfast, dinner and what had to be every meal she'd ever eaten present itself in reverse order.

"Oh god, Adalia," Trent hurried into the bathroom and stroked her back. "It's okay, I'm here."

She didn't have the strength to wave him away. So much for romance on their honeymoon. She spent another two minutes in the same state, then flushed the toilet and collapsed against the wall.

Why was everything white in this damn place?

Trent handed her a couple squares of toilet paper and she dabbed at the corners of her mouth. "I'm sorry," she mumbled, "I didn't expect that to happen."

"Don't say sorry, Adalia. It's not like you can help it. I'm worried about you… this looks like food poisoning. We should go see a doctor." He cupped her cheek in his palm and tilted his head to the side, bright blue eyes brimming with concern.

Adalia could barely lift her head. She was exhausted and sweaty, and God, she just wanted a glass of water and a good sleep.

"Don't be ridic –" She pushed him back and vomited noisily into the toilet again. Where could all this have come from –? She'd surely puked out everything else.

"That's it. We're going to see a doctor." Trent rose and hurried into the living room.

Adalia flushed again and struggled into the standing position, then shuffled to the sink. She grasped her cheeks and slapped them to take away the numbness. What the hell was this?

She'd read an article once about eating yogurt to get the local bacteria when visiting a new country, but this was insane. She'd hardly had a chance to unpack. Hell, she'd eaten nothing since they'd arrived, not even a sip of damned champagne.

Adalia brushed her teeth, then washed her mouth out and gargled. That would have to do for now – there was no helping the clammy hands and weak knees.

Trent appeared in the doorway. "Are you done?"

"Yeah, I'm okay. Trent, we really don't need to go to the doctor. It's just a bug… it will pass."

"Like hell it will. Let's go. There's a doctor just around the corner." He guided her from the bathroom with a smile and a gentle caress in the small of her back.

***

Dr. Michelakis had a moustache to rival Yosemite Sam, and deep brown eyes which expressed a lot of sympathy. He tugged on one of the face caterpillars and leaned forward.

"What's the problem?" he asked, in his thick Greek accent.

Adalia leaned back in the plastic chair at the front of his desk and laid her hands over her belly. "I've got a tummy bug or something. I keep throwing up and I feel a bit sweaty and weak."

The good doctor squeaked back in his chair and studied her, gaze sweeping over her belly and then to Trent.

"Alright. We take urine and blood sample, then we check to see the problem."

"How long will it take until we know what's wrong?" Trent asked, grasping Adalia's knee and running his thumb along the outside of her thigh.

"Maybe hour or two. Our lab is empty of samples now, so should go very, very quickly." Dr. Michelakis rose and walked to the door. He opened it and shouted something in Greek, then walked back to his desk. "Nurse is coming now to take your blood sample." He slapped a plastic receptacle onto the table and smiled at Adalia. "You make a pee in this one now."

What a charmer. She nodded to him and snatched up the plastic container, then hurried out of the room and to the restroom across the hall. Five minutes later, she was back in his office with a vial of yellow fluid. A nurse was waiting, holding a needle and a syringe.

"Is this really necessary?" she asked. "It's just the flu or stomach bug."

"Just let the nurse do what she has to do, Adalia," Trent advised.

She shot him a venomous look. He wasn't the one who had to get holes poked in him by a trigger happy Greek nurse with a nose that could've climbed trees.

The bloodletting was done in another fifteen minutes and Adalia settled in to wait. They'd decided to hang around in the doctor's office. Actually, Trent had decided they weren't going anywhere until they knew what was wrong with her and how to fix it.

"You're blowing this out of proportion," she grunted. "So what if I have food poisoning? I'll throw up a couple times and stay in bed for a day or two. It's not a big deal."

"Of course it's a big deal," he snapped, "I want you to enjoy our honeymoon, not be confined to the bedroom. At least not under this pretext. God, Adalia. Don't you care about your own health?"

"Don't start on me, I'm not in the mood," she said.

The office was empty. The doctor had popped out to catch a quick lunch. Apparently, things moved slowly in Santorini, and his afternoon was clear except for the blood and urine tests.

She grabbed the bottle of water Trent had bought for her and unscrewed the cap. She swigged a few gulps then pulled a face at the resurgence of nausea.

"What is it? Do you need to go to the bathroom? Are you going to throw up again?" he rattled off the questions in rapid succession.

"Oh my God!" Adalia slammed the bottle onto the table top. "Would you fucking relax? You're starting to get on my nerves now."

"I'm just looking out for you," he said, his tone turning sullen. He looked out the window and silence fell between them.

Oh well, it was better than constant questions and concerns. She'd never seen him this way before. He was terrified for her safety, yet there was nothing seriously wrong with her. Trent had revealed a different side to himself, a more vulnerable side. Maybe if she hadn't been about to toss her cookies all over the desk, she would have found it endearing.

The door cracked open behind them and Trent straightened and turned. Adalia stared dead ahead, seething for God alone knew what reason. Because Trent cared enough to rush her to a doctor? That was a good trait, so why did it piss her off this much?

"Ah good, you still here." Dr. Michelakis entered and bustled to his desk, carrying a brown folder and a moustache coated in bread crumbs. He took a seat and brushed the remains of his lunch away from his lips.

"So, what's the verdict?" Trent asked, before Adalia could say a word.

"Yes, what's wrong with me?" Adalia followed up, casting another expression of irritation at her husband. What a way to spend their first day as a married couple.

"Is very simple. I look at the urine sample first and find out the result, but want to confirm with blood test." The doctor opened the file and slid two pieces of paper onto his desk. He positioned his elbows on the wood surface, balled up his fists and pressed them into his cheeks while studying the results.

"And that means what?" Adalia tapped her foot impatiently. She wanted to get home and nap as soon as possible.

"It means what I suspected. You are going to have a baby." He spread his arms wide, then made a cradle and rocked it from side to side. "Congratulations. Such a lovely surprise."

"What?!" Adalia spat. "You're kidding, right? I'm pregnant? I'm getting sick because I'm pregnant. Is this some kind of joke?"

"No joke. You no worry, this is good news for you. Good news about little baby." Dr. Michelakis stood and gestured to the door.

Adalia couldn't bring herself to stand. "I'm pregnant."

"Yes, now have good afternoon. You take the vitamins." He scratched out a prescription on a piece of paper and handed it to Trent. He accepted it, expression completely blank.

Adalia's mind was a mess of emotions and thoughts. How was this possible?

She didn't look at Trent all the way to the drug store. They got back to the hotel and she walked into the bedroom and closed the door, then climbed right into bed, gripping her stomach.

If you enjoyed this sample then look for **Love Endured: Tenacious Billionaire BWWM Romance Series, Book 3**.

Here is a preview of **another book** you may also enjoy:

Love Restrained - Fervent Billionaire BWWM Romance Series, Book 2

ALEXA STARED at the bright white of the computer screen. It seemed to be mocking her with its very emptiness. She sighed. If she did not start on her freelance work soon, she would never get done. With a groan, she stood up and went to the kitchen for a cup of coffee. She decided to take a much-needed break before she started the workday. Alexa glanced at the clock. Already, it was approaching ten in the morning. Today was a waste. All she needed to do was look up the keywords needed for a client's blog. That was it. Leaning back against the counter, she tried to refocus her mind on work. Nothing helped. Since her fling with William a month ago, she had been unable to focus on anything. It was amazing that one little date could change her entire outlook.

The ringing of the phone snapped her back to the present. Crossing the room, she picked it up and answered. The number was not familiar, but many of the clients she used called her on this line. It could be important or it could be a spammer. In her line of work, either option was equally likely.

"Hello?" she asked. "Alexandria Enterprise. How may I direct your call?"

A laugh was heard on the other end of the line and Alexa groaned. It was her mother. "Now don't you Alexandria me, young lady. I gave birth to you and I know as well as anybody that you are no Alexandria."

Alexa rolled her eyes. Vividly alive and slightly domineering, her mother was a veritable force of nature. Alexa had named her company Alexandria as a reference to the old libraries that burned in Alexandria. The metaphor was lost on her mother, however. "Yes, Mama, I know. Ten hours of labor and what did you get?"

"A daughter who puts on airs," her mother finished.

Alexa sighed. "So what is it this time, Mama? You fixing me up with Sammy again? He's gay, you know. Just because you and his mom don't believe it..." she trailed off. It was useless arguing. Her mother had noticed Alexa's lack of a love life and spent the last month trying to fix her up with men from the neighborhood. Alexa groaned inwardly. Men. No, the men of the neighborhood had been snatched up a long time ago. What was left was a mix of boys who could never compete. The only person she would have even considered dating was Sammy, but he had other interests that did not involve slender hips and voluptuous breasts.

"No, no, Alexa. I won't be fixing you up with anyone this time. I just want to see you every once in a while. Dinner with me tonight? I'll cook your favorite… fried chicken."

Sighing, Alexa nodded. She instantly realized that her mother couldn't see her nod, so she replied, "Sure, Mama. That's fine. I'll see you around six."

Hanging up the phone, Alexa went back to her desk. She would have to complete a great deal of work before driving down to Tacoma. Even worse, she was going to be suckered into eating her mother's extremely delicious and exceptionally fattening chicken. So much for giving up fried food.

After she sat down at the desk, the minutes quickly fled by. Alexa became engrossed in the project and barely noticed that the light was starting to dim from the sky. Glancing up, she realized that it was already 4 PM. Thankfully, she was done. Leaning back from the computer, she reached over and picked her phone on the first ring.

"Hello, Alexandria Enterprises."

"Hey... Alexa? This is you, right?" The voice on the phone caused her to sit up straight. She recognized the deep, gravelly voice.

"William? What... What do you want?" She winced. Her attempt at playing it cool already failed.

"Nothing, Alexa, at least not in the way you're thinking." He paused as he tried to figure out how to word his question. "Well, I remember you talking about marketing and the internet at our... dinner." Alexa did not say anything, so William continued. "Anyhow, I think I may want to utilize your services. When would you be available?"

Alexa picked up her schedule. Normally, she would tell him that she did not work with friends, but considering that they had only spent an evening together, she could ignore her normal rule. Not to mention that he would probably end up being one of her major clients. "Yes, yes, I could do that. How about we arrange for a consultation in..." She flipped through her schedule. "Two weeks?"

"Two weeks? Wow, business must be going well. Yes, we could do that. Let me put my secretary on the line and she will handle the scheduling aspect. I'll tell you more about what I want in person."

If you enjoyed this sample then look for **Love Restrained - Fervent Billionaire BWWM Romance Series, Book 2**.

Here is a preview of **another book** you may also enjoy:

"**ARE WE** doing spring cleaning?" Markey Green asked his sister Chante as he eyed the clothes strewn all over her bedroom floor.

"What? No…no…no…" Chante replied, as she pulled another hanger from inside her clothes drawer.

"I just need to find the right one…" she added as she positioned the dress in front of her and stared at her reflection in the mirror.

She shook her head in disapproval. "Too revealing," she muttered under her breathe.

Markey advanced slowly into his sister's bedroom. He didn't want his wheelchair to run into the dresses that were piled haphazardly on the floor.

"Must be a hot date then," he smiled with amusement as his sister began to attack the shelves where her shoes rested.

Chante stopped momentarily. She was surprised at her brother's spontaneous perception. She smiled trying to mask the concern in her eyes. He had grown so much thinner these last few months. His ALS had progressed so much faster than she thought.

"And what do you know about having a hot date, hmmm…" she said as she tousled his hair.

"Well…enough to notice that you're excited once again. These last few months you just seemed… sad." Markey replied.

Chante felt a twinge of guilt. She honestly didn't realize her brother noticed at all.

"Was I that bad…" she asked as she sat down on the bed.

"Bad? Nah, you were just sad." Markey answered wryly.

"Yeah, I guess I was…but I'm ok now…so don't you worry about me kid." Chante replied.

She never told him about the way she felt. In fact she hasn't told anyone about it. Who would believe her anyway? It isn't every day that a good-looking and wealthy... very wealthy... Jared Lowell asked you to be his sex toy.

Chante tried to forget everything that happened that day on the roof deck of NY General Hospital. She remembered him calling her name as she pushed the metal doors aside and ran towards the freight elevator. She punched the button on the lift and went all the way to the basement where she knew she would be safe. She was confused, her mind was in a whirl, and she wanted to stay away from prying eyes. She stopped by a wall and there amidst rows of empty cars she slumped down on the hard cement floor as despair and disillusionment brought waves of tears that shook her to the core.

"How dare him…" she muttered disconsolately, "he must think I'm scum."

Jared Lowell, heir to the fortunes of Lowell Enterprises had just offered to keep her as a mistress in exchange for a condo and for "stuff" as he called it, even having the impudence to conclude "that's what girls like…"

But Chante didn't have the heart to put all the censure on the scoundrel. She was partly to blame too, remembering what happened between them in the bathroom of the suite where his mother was a patient.

"Shit…" she whispered between her tears.

But it was too late now for regrets. It happened and she had to live with it. In hindsight, she was confused why she even allowed it to come about. Had the patient, Samantha Lowell, or Nurse Betty, and Director Whittle come back and caught them in the illicit act, she would have lost her job as Certified Nursing Assistant, that's for sure.

It was with uncertainty that she reported for work the very next day. She had vowed the night before that she would refuse adamantly, beg even, not to be assigned to Suite 247 once again. But the floor seemed unusually quiet that morning. She learned that Samantha Lowell was discharged the night before. The private helicopter that brought her in brought her out, as well.

"Oh, thank God," was Chante's initial reaction.

She didn't have to suffer the awkwardness of seeing Jared again. Admittedly, she liked Mrs. Lowell. She felt a certain degree of kinship with the older woman. It made her a little sad, thinking she didn't get a chance to say goodbye.

But as the initial relief swept through her body, she was also assailed with a deep sense of melancholy. She won't be seeing Jared Lowell anymore. That, at least, was its own blessing, Chante thought.

The weeks that followed their departure, Chante often had to struggle with her feelings. She tried to focus on her work but often found herself looking out into space. She felt miserable, disconnected, and it took all her effort to keep going about her duty. The world lay heavily on her shoulders.

Nurse Betty took her aside and asked what was bothering her. Chante couldn't look her in the eye. The woman was very perceptive.

"Is this about a man?" Nurse Betty inquired.

Chante nodded her head. The supervisor didn't have to know who. So Chante decided on a half-lie.

"Yes…but it's over now…" Chante answered.

"That's good. If it didn't last too long, then he must be the wrong guy for you. Get out of that hole you crawled into. Someone better should come along for you." The supervisor consoled her.

Chante nodded her head in agreement. Nurse Betty didn't know how close to the truth she was. Jared

Lowell was definitely the wrong guy for her. It's about time she moved on and forgot all about him.

Things were slowly getting back to normal.

If you enjoyed this sample then look for **Love Astray: Audacious Billionaire BWWM Romance Series, Book 2**.

Other Books by Shyla Starr

- Persuasive Billionaire BWWM Romance Series

- Elusive Billionaire Romance Series

- Lonely Billionaire Romance Series

- Ardent Billionaire Romance Series

- Fervent Billionaire BWWM Romance Series

- Audacious Billionaire BWWM Romance Series

Get the latest update on new releases from the author at:

https://shylastarr.com/newsletter/

About the Author - Shyla Starr

Shyla currently specializes in writing interracial romance stories and is a huge fan of the alpha male. Simply put, there just aren't enough stories about mixed couple romances, which is something she is aiming to fix.

Being a bookworm all her life, when Shyla discovered men she also realized how easy it was to fulfill her fantasies through her writing.

When not writing and fantasizing about men, Shyla enjoys dancing, reading and chilling with her friends.

Connect with Shyla Starr

I really appreciate you reading my book! Here are my social media coordinates:

Friend me on Facebook:
https://www.facebook.com/shylastarrauthor

Follow me on Twitter: https://twitter.com/shylstarr

Check me out on Goodreads:
https://www.goodreads.com/author/show/8436084.Shyla_Starr

Subscribe to my newsletter:
https://shylastarr.com/newsletter/

Visit my website: https://shylastarr.com/

www.ingramcontent.com/pod-product-compliance
Lightning Source LLC
Chambersburg PA
CBHW021336190726
48288CB00003B/1130